What was Casey
happened to tur

A soft knock on the study door pulled his thoughts back. "Come in," he said.

Casey stood in the doorway. "Dinner's ready."

No salutation, small talk or frivolous chatter. The devil of it was that she couldn't be further from his type. Casey Thomas was all buttoned-down efficiency and he couldn't stop thinking about unbuttoning her. How stupid was that?

He was her employer and an attorney. Any move on his part in that direction was inappropriate, not to mention would open the door for a sexual harassment lawsuit.

"Blake? I'm going to get Mia."

His niece.

The whole reason Casey was there.

Dear Reader,

The family dynamic is both complicated and emotional. When a relative dies, especially at a young age, the loss is deeper and more devastating, the "what ifs" more emotional, the "if onlys" more sad.

I grew up a middle child, one of six siblings. Like Blake Decker in *The Nanny and Me,* I lost my only sister to cancer when she was thirty-six years old. This shared loss brought my four brothers and me even closer, but there are certain things the guys will never understand the way my sister did. Like the vital importance of a gifted hairstylist. Or the critical need to keep a pedicure appointment.

No one can replace my sister, but through a shared love of storytelling I've been fortunate enough to meet bright, funny women who have become like sisters to me. And being part of the Silhouette Special Edition family is an honor and privilege—not to mention a dream come true. I have the best job in the world thanks to you awesome readers.

Happy reading!

Teresa Southwick

THE NANNY
AND ME

TERESA SOUTHWICK

SPECIAL EDITION®

Published by Silhouette Books

America's Publisher of Contemporary Romance

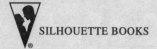

SILHOUETTE BOOKS

ISBN-13: 978-0-373-65483-3

THE NANNY AND ME

Recycling programs
for this product may
not exist in your area.

Copyright © 2009 by Teresa Ann Southwick

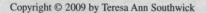

Visit Silhouette Books at www.eHarlequin.com

Printed in U.S.A.

Books by Teresa Southwick

Silhouette Special Edition

The Summer House #1510
 "Courting Cassandra"
Midnight, Moonlight &
 Miracles #1517
It Takes Three #1631
~The Beauty Queen's Makeover #1699
At the Millionaire's Request #1769
§§Paging Dr. Daddy #1886
‡The Millionaire and the M.D. #1894
‡When a Hero Comes Along #1905
‡Expecting the Doctor's Baby #1924
‡‡Marrying the Virgin Nanny #1960
‡The Doctor's Secret Baby #1982
‡The Nanny and Me #2001

Silhouette Books

The Fortunes of Texas:
 Shotgun Vows

Silhouette Romance

Wedding Rings and
 Baby Things #1209
The Bachelor's Baby #1233
*A Vow, a Ring, a Baby Swing #1349
The Way to a Cowboy's Heart #1383
*And Then He Kissed Me #1405
*With a Little T.L.C. #1421
The Acquired Bride #1474
*Secret Ingredient: Love #1495
*The Last Marchetti Bachelor #1513
**Crazy for Lovin' You #1529
**This Kiss #1541
**If You Don't Know by Now #1560
**What If We Fall in Love? #1572
Sky Full of Promise #1624
†To Catch a Sheik #1674
†To Kiss a Sheik #1686
†To Wed a Sheik #1696

††Baby, Oh Baby #1704
††Flirting with the Boss #1708
††An Heiress on His
 Doorstep #1712
§That Touch of Pink #1799
§In Good Company #1807
§Something's Gotta Give #1815

*The Marchetti Family
**Destiny, Texas
†Desert Brides
††If Wishes Were…
§Buy-a-Guy
~Most Likely To…
§§The Wilder Family
‡The Men of Mercy Medical
‡‡The Nanny Network

TERESA SOUTHWICK

lives with her husband in Las Vegas, the city that reinvents itself every day. An avid fan of romance novels, she is delighted to be living out her dream of writing for Silhouette Books.

For Taelor and Jensen Southwick,
who suggested the name for the dog in this story.
Girls, you're beautiful inside and out.

Chapter One

No one liked to be made a fool of and Casey Thomas had reason to hate it more than most. The last time someone did it, her best friend had died.

The last thing she needed was manipulation from her boss.

And what a boss she was. Ginger Davis was a beautiful brunette who proved that fifty really was the new thirty and not just a marketing phrase. The president and CEO of the Las Vegas-based Nanny Network had to be on the far side of forty-nine but didn't look anywhere close to that. Apparently she thrived on the stress generated by managing the exclusive, expensive company specializing in child care for the rich and famous.

Casey glared across the glass-topped desk in her boss's home office. "This could have been handled over the phone, Ginger. You insisted I come here because you don't think I can tell you no to your face."

Ginger folded her hands, then rested them on a stack of files, her expression not the least bit apologetic. "I wanted you to meet Blake Decker and his *orphaned* niece and tell him no to *his* face."

If that wasn't blatant manipulation, Casey would eat her *Child Rearing for Dummies* handbook. The woman just had to get the word *orphaned* in there. It wasn't that Casey was unsympathetic. She'd lost her own mother when she was eleven. But as a nanny, she had rules—and good reasons for them.

She had the physical and emotional scars to prove that undoing a system of beliefs ingrained over many years was a losing proposition and a waste of time and energy. Army service had taught her that life was unpredictable and whatever time one had on this earth should not be squandered by spitting into the wind. If she was going to help a child, it would be in the child's formative years, before negative influences took hold.

"You know my focus is on children under ten years old."

Her boss nodded. "And you know that my job is to pair up my employees with clients who are a good fit. You're happy. The client is happy. Everyone is happy."

Casey wasn't feeling the love. "Is this where we link arms and sing 'Kumbaya'?"

"If that works for you." Ginger smiled. "Casey, I know what happened to you overseas while you were in the service. And I understand why you specialize in a certain age group. I've respected your boundaries without question since you joined the Nanny Network family."

Owing this woman was darned inconvenient. Ginger had taken her on after she'd been medically discharged from the army. Casey had received on-the-job training in the preschool Nooks and Nannies and was now working for the Nanny Network while taking early childhood development classes to finish up her elementary school teaching credential.

She was a live-in nanny, caring for children ten and under, giving them a stable base of operations and showing them how to be upstanding human beings through example, discipline and love. The career was incredibly rewarding. And she needed all the rewarding she could get to fill up her redemption jar. When a friend paid with their life because of you, going on with your own life wasn't easy.

Still, she was trying to make a difference as best she could. Why did Ginger have to put her on the spot? Why couldn't Ginger let her continue to do what she loved to do on her own terms?

"I'm already working for the Redmonds."

"You have a break for the next month, while they're in Europe with Heidi and Jack. I'll have a replacement when they return."

The truth was, Casey had been dreading having too much time on her hands to think. That didn't mean she was willing to bend her rules. "I have plans for my time off."

"And I need to ask you to cancel them as a favor to me. This little girl is twelve—only two years over your bottom line. She's a kid who needs a break."

Casey knew she was going to hate herself for asking but couldn't stop the words. "Why should I make an exception for Blake Decker and his orphaned niece?"

"See for yourself." Ginger hit her intercom and asked her assistant to send them in.

There was very little wiggle room between a rock and a hard place, and Casey hated that, too.

Moments after the summons a man came into the office with a young girl strolling behind him. He walked right up to Casey, who was still standing in front of Ginger's desk.

"Blake Decker," he said.

"Casey Thomas," she answered, shaking the hand he held out.

He looked at the girl beside him. "This is my niece Mia Decker."

"Nice to meet you, Mia."

"Yeah. Whatever."

The child barely made eye contact. In her threadbare jeans, multilayered T-shirts and zippered cardigan sweatshirt, which was hanging off her shoulders, she was the picture of bored indifference. She was also a beautiful little girl with long, wavy brown hair and huge eyes that were an unusual shade of blue-green, almost turquoise.

Apparently the remarkable Decker DNA was liberally spread around. Her uncle was an exceptionally good-looking man somewhere in his mid- to late thirties. Casey had seen her share of hunks in the army, but this guy's dark hair, blue eyes and square jaw could fill movie theater seats around the world.

The dark charcoal suit, red tie and white shirt fit his tall, lean body perfectly and looked expensive. Instinct told her that he could afford the Nanny Network's upscale price tag, but so far she hadn't seen any reason to make an exception to her personal rules. Not even the fact that he looked like he wanted to wring his niece's neck for her rudeness and attitude.

"I'm sorry for Mia's bad manners," he finally said.

"And I'm sorry you're such a dork," Mia shot back.

Ginger cleared her throat. "Why don't you both sit down and everyone can get better acquainted."

"What for?" Mia asked. "He's just going to dump me like everyone else."

Her uncle shifted uncomfortably. "Mia, I'm not going to dump you—"

"Define *everyone*," Casey said.

The girl stared angrily at her. "Why do you care?"

"I don't," Casey answered honestly. The last thing this kid

needed was an adult patronizing her. "I don't know you well enough to have an emotional investment in you."

"Then why are you asking questions?" Mia demanded.

"Call it curiosity."

"I'm not show-and-tell," the kid snapped. "This is all just stupid—"

"Mia—" Blake's cell phone rang and he pulled it from the case at his waist. After looking at the caller ID, he replaced the phone and let the call go to voice mail. He shot his niece a stern look as he stared down at her. "Miss Davis asked you to sit."

Mia glared defiantly for several moments, then apparently decided that arguing about this wasn't a hill she wanted to die on. Without a word she flopped into a chair, although her body language was anything but silent. The slouch and scowl said loud and clear that every adult in the room was a complete moron.

In spite of herself, Casey was getting sucked in, and apparently her boss knew and planned to capitalize on the weakness.

The first clue was when Ginger stood and said, "I'm going to let the three of you talk. I have some calls to make and I'll just step into the other room to do that."

Before Casey could protest, they were alone. She wanted to end this meeting and walk out, too, but the girl's words had struck a nerve. "You didn't answer my question, Mia. Who else dumped you?"

"My niece has had a tough time," Blake said for Mia. "My sister wasn't in a good place and never developed the instincts or skills to handle her. There's no point in going over all that."

Casey looked up at him, way up. "First of all, Mr. Decker, my question was directed to Mia." She glanced at the girl and noticed something in her eyes. It vanished almost instantly, but for just a moment interest had replaced the bored look. "Secondly, may I ask what you do for a living?"

"I'm an attorney."

"Family law?"

"Not exactly."

"What exactly?" Casey asked.

"Divorce." He met her gaze but it was impossible to tell what he was thinking.

"I see." She looked at the child. "Are you going to answer my question?"

"Do I have to?" Mia glared.

"Yes." Casey folded her arms and looked down, letting Mia know she was prepared to wait as long as necessary.

"I forgot what it was."

"Who else dumped you?" Casey repeated.

After several moments, Mia huffed out an exasperated breath. "My father split before I was born. My mother died. I stayed with his sister for a while but she didn't want me."

"It's not that black-and-white," her uncle said.

"Sure it is," Mia shot back, her beautiful eyes spitting anger and resentment. "No one wants me. Including you."

The words touched Casey somewhere deep inside and she looked at the girl. "Mia, would you mind waiting for your uncle in the other room?"

"Why?"

"Because I'd like to speak with him alone." Casey met the defiant gaze and said wryly, "What have you got to lose? This is all stupid, anyway. Right?"

Her full cupid's bow mouth pulled into a straight line before Mia snapped, "Whatever."

She stomped out of the room and slammed the door.

Casey leaned back against the glass-topped desk as she looked at the uncle. "If it's not black-and-white, there must be shades of gray, Mr. Decker. Tell me about your niece."

He unbuttoned his suit jacket and rested his hands on lean

hips. "It's an old story, Miss Thomas. My sister got involved with the wrong guy. She got pregnant. My parents threw her out and she disappeared. I was away at college and never heard from her. I didn't even know I had a niece until Child Protective Services recently contacted me. There's no one else to take her."

The kid was right. He didn't want her, either. "You could let her go into the state system."

"No."

"Why not?"

"That's a good question." His phone rang again, and when he looked at the number, he said, "Excuse me. I have to take this." Flipping the phone open, he snapped, "What?" After listening, he nodded. "I'll be there in a half hour. It's a deposition. They can wait." He ended the call and replaced the phone in its case, never taking his gaze from hers. "You want to know why I took her in and I wish I had an answer. It could be as simple as the fact that she's family, but it doesn't feel that way. She's a stranger. All I can tell you for sure is that she's not going to Child Protective Services."

Casey respected his honesty a lot more than she wanted to. She wished he were a complete jerk, which would make it easy to tell him to take a flying leap. Instead she asked, "Why do you need a nanny?"

"I have to work." He ran his fingers through his hair. "It's safe to say that I have no idea how to raise any child, let alone a girl. She's too young to leave unsupervised."

"There are after-school programs." Casey could feel her resolve weakening. *Darn Ginger.* She was right about telling him no to his face. The rock and the hard place were putting the squeeze on her. "I'd be happy to recommend activities that will give her supervision while you work."

"First of all, my workday is longer than your after-school

activities." He blew out a long breath. "Second, don't pretend that she's your average, normal twelve-year-old girl. She needs more than arts and crafts and a field trip to the zoo."

"What does she need?"

"You tell me. That's your area of expertise." He held his hands out in a helpless gesture that looked like it didn't fit, like it was foreign to him. "If you were a client wanting to dissolve your marriage, I would be the legal professional you'd consult."

"But I'm not." She'd never been married. Came close once, but it didn't happen. She wasn't marriage material. Marriage required trust and that was blasted out of her by a suicide bomber in Iraq.

He met her gaze and there was something almost desperate in his own. "My point is that a good lawyer knows when he is out of his depth and needs to consult an expert. Specifically, I need an expert on children. The Nanny Network comes highly recommended and Miss Davis tells me you're the expert I need to consult."

This man was asking her to intervene on behalf of an obviously troubled girl and she didn't want to go there again. Her judgment couldn't be trusted and it wasn't fair to either of them for her to agree to the arrangement.

"Did she also tell you that I don't accept clients over a certain age?"

"Yes. I asked her to prevail upon you to make an exception in Mia's case."

"I can't do that. I'm sorry." She straightened away from the desk. "Ginger has a lot of contacts. I'm sure she can help you find someone."

"She already found you and she tells me you're highly qualified for Mia's needs. I'd really like you to think it over," he said.

So she'd finally told him no to his face and he didn't understand the meaning of the word. Casey walked to the door and opened it. "I've already made up my mind."

She glanced around, expecting to see a hostile Mia slouched in a chair, with antagonism rolling off her like sound waves. Instead the room was empty.

Blake Decker needed this like a brain aneurysm. He had back-to-back appointments stacked up like planes waiting to land and was due in court after lunch for a high-profile celebrity client whose wife had been caught cheating by the paparazzi. Mia couldn't have picked a worse day to do a disappearing act.

In the elevator, he glanced down at Casey. "You don't need to help look for her."

"No. But two pairs of eyes are better than one."

When the elevator reached the ground floor, the doors whooshed open and he held out a hand, indicating she should precede him. They hurried across the lobby of the luxurious high-rise building and walked outside, then scanned up and down the sidewalk, looking for a glimpse of Mia.

"Do you see her?" he asked.

Casey stood on tiptoe, trying to see around the pedestrians strolling past. "That green sweatshirt she was wearing will stand out, but I don't see it."

Blake wondered how this day had gone so horribly wrong. Technically, things had started south when Mia came to live with him a couple weeks ago. Since then his days and nights had been a nightmare of calls from school regarding tardiness and skipped classes, of not knowing where the kid was half the time, and of wondering what she was doing while he was at work.

He was a lawyer. He was good at it and understood the law.

As his niece's legal guardian, he was responsible for her behavior and liable for her mistakes. The buck stopped here. His life hadn't been this screwed up since he caught his wife sleeping with his best friend.

He looked down at Casey. "I appreciate the gesture, but she's my problem. I'll find her."

"Don't look a gift horse in the mouth."

The gesture was definitely a gift, because she had turned down his offer of a job and wasn't on the clock. Another way his day had gone south. He wasn't accustomed to losing a negotiation.

He studied the shadows in her big hazel eyes. Casey was an attractive blonde with silky hair cut in choppy layers that skimmed her shoulders—messy, straight, sharp, sexy layers. And shoulders. The white sundress showed off bare arms that were as tanned and toned as her great legs. Her sandals revealed toes painted a vivid shade of red.

What he could see told him she kept in shape and that shape was better than good. But it was nothing compared to her mouth. He could hardly keep himself from staring at her full lips. They were no doubt a result of an amazing gift from her gene pool, because she didn't seem like the cosmetic injection type. And the deep dimples in her cheeks flashed when she was annoyed, which made him wonder how they'd look with a smile, which so far he hadn't seen. She was no-nonsense, no pretense, no games. No compunction about turning down his job offer. Yet here she was, pounding the pavement with him.

"Why do you feel the need to help?" he asked.

"I sent her out of the room. I feel responsible for her taking off. She's obviously upset—"

His cell phone rang and he recognized the office number. "Hi, Rita. I know I'm late." He listened to the list of appointments, although it was a waste of breath. He already knew his day was screwed thanks to Mia. "Look, something's come up. I need you to cancel my appointments and reschedule." He glanced at his watch. "With luck I'll make it to court. If not, I'll let you know so Leo can fill in. You're a lifesaver, Ree. Thanks."

"You're a busy man," Casey commented.

He nodded. "My niece picked the worst possible time to crank up the rebellion."

"Like I was saying," she said pointedly, "Mia's obviously upset."

"How can you tell? What you saw was normal for her. Since I took her in, sarcastic, abrasive and belligerent have been the full range of her disposition." He looked up and down the street without spotting the familiar green sweatshirt. "And I think it's safe to add unpredictable to that list."

"It's not really a surprise, given the instability in her life. We're all a product of our environment, Mr. Decker—"

"Call me Blake."

She nodded, then continued. "I sent her out of the room and that makes me feel a certain responsibility for her taking off. The least I can do is help you find her."

The seriously stubborn look on her face told him he couldn't talk her out of this, and truthfully, he was grateful for the company. "Okay. Thanks."

"You're welcome."

As they walked and talked, her gaze scanned left and right, as if they were on patrol. He remembered a detail of her résumé, one that made her come-and-get-me red-painted toes even more intriguing. "Miss Davis said you were in the army."

"That's right."

He waited for her to elaborate, but she didn't. "She thought your background would make you a good fit for Mia. Strong and smart enough to handle her."

"Ginger is wrong."

He studied the tension in her shoulders and mouth. He knew the basics of her military experience but had a feeling there was a sad story in there somewhere. She had the sexiest lips this side of heaven and the saddest eyes he'd ever seen. Sad stories and broken dreams were his stock-in-trade. He'd lived his own and made a fortune on other people's. This woman touched a nerve with him and that hadn't happened for a long time. It wasn't a good thing.

So maybe it was for the best that Casey had refused to work for him. On the other hand, the more time he spent with her, the more convinced he became that her boss was right about her being strong enough to deal with Mia.

Down the street from the corporate office of the Nanny Network, they stopped at a traffic light. Fashion Show Mall was across the street, and there was still no sign of Mia.

"Maybe we should call the police," Blake said.

"We will if we have to but let's keep looking."

"Any ideas where we should look?"

Casey looked at him, her expression part wryness, part pity. She nodded her head toward the upscale shopping center. "If I wanted to lose myself, that's where I'd go. Retail therapy works wonders."

He nodded. "I see the 'duh' look in your eyes. I believe I already confessed to knowing zero about a twelve-year-old girl."

"And what makes you think I do?"

"You were twelve once and you're female. That puts you one up on me." The look in her eyes said it was a long time ago. "Little girls are way beyond my range of experience."

"Big girls are more your style?"

"I like women, if that's what you're asking. But my style? I don't have one." He shook his head. "For the record, I don't think any man understands them. Young, old or anywhere in between, women are the eighth wonder of the world and as mysterious as the elusive commodity of luck in this town."

She put a hand to her forehead, shading her eyes from the sun. "I'm not sure how to respond to that, so I won't. But I say we go check out the mall."

"Okay."

After crossing at the light, they followed the sidewalk and entered the mall at the food court on the third level. He shadowed Casey when she headed for the escalator. That was when he realized she moved pretty fast for a woman who wasn't all that tall. She was maybe a couple inches over five feet. Blake was six feet two and had a long stride, but when they got off on a lower floor, she had no trouble keeping up with him. They marched past Nordstrom, Dillard's, Neiman Marcus, Saks Fifth Avenue and every small, upscale store in between. On the first level they did the same thing, without spotting Mia.

In the center of the mall he stopped to look around. "I think maybe it's time to call the police."

She was studying a graphic of the mall's layout. "Okay."

He started to pull out his cell when she took off. "I thought we were getting the cops involved."

"We are. In a manner of speaking."

Blake trailed after her to the mall security office. Inside there was a twentysomething guy in navy trousers and a light blue shirt with an official mall security patch on the sleeve. Blake saw a familiar girl in a green sweatshirt sitting by the desk.

"Mia." He let out a long breath, then explained that she was his niece and he was her legal guardian.

Rent-a-cop gave Mia an unsympathetic look. "She was caught stealing makeup."

The Bonnie Parker wannabe had been gone for what?

Twenty minutes? A half hour tops? It hadn't taken her long to get in trouble. Probably he should be grateful that she wasn't good enough at being bad to get away with it, but that was small comfort.

Blake knew the law, but everyone had a specialty and criminal law wasn't his. When all else failed, it couldn't hurt to bluff. "I'm guessing that pressing charges would be more costly and time-consuming than it's worth. What if I give you my word that you won't see her in here again?" He looked at Mia, who was trying to look sullen, but a little bit of fright leaked through. "And there will be consequences for her at home." That part was *really* a bluff, because he had no idea what those consequences would be.

"Okay." The security guy frowned at Blake's niece. "You got off easy, kid."

Blake nodded. "Thanks. I'll make sure she doesn't do anything like this again."

Right after he flapped his arms and landed on the moon, because he had no clue how to keep that promise.

With Mia between them, Blake and Casey walked back toward the mall entrance.

"I have to go to the bathroom," Mia said when they passed the restrooms.

Was this another escape attempt? Could he trust her not to take off again?

As if Casey could read his thoughts, she said, "I'll check it out."

She disappeared into the ladies' room and was back in a moment. "Clear," she said.

Mia did a dramatic eye roll but held back any sarcastic comment as she went in.

Blake studied the door that said Women. "Maybe I can get her one of those electronic surveillance devices for her ankle."

"You're not very good at this, are you?"

He sighed. "You have no idea how badly I'd like to say 'Duh.' That's what I've been trying to tell you. I freely admit that I need help. It's why I tried to hire you in the first place."

She nodded without saying anything, but it was almost as if he could see the conflict raging inside her. Doubts darted across her face and highlighted the uncertainty in her eyes, but finally she met his gaze.

"Do you still want me to work for you?" she asked.

"Is the pope Catholic? Do bears go anywhere they want in the woods?"

A half smile curved up the corners of her mouth. "Is that a yes?"

"That's as close to a yes as I can get without begging," he confirmed.

"Okay. I'll accept the position on a trial basis. If it doesn't work out—"

He touched a finger to her lips to silence her. "Think positive."

That was his plan and he wasn't an especially positive kind of guy. However, he was positive that brushing her lips just now had made him want to explore them even further. That was pretty stupid, after she'd finally agreed to work for him.

Still, considering his history with women, stupid was pretty much in character for him. Since his marriage imploded, he'd learned to expect the worst, because that way he never got blindsided.

Right now he chose to hope for the best with his new nanny, because he really needed her.

Chapter Two

Casey stood at the door to Blake Decker's penthouse, located at One Queensridge Place, and fervently wished for a decision do-over. He'd said he specialized in divorce law, and judging by his living arrangements, there was an obscene amount of money in marriages gone bad. The lobby of this luxury building had all dark wood walls, crystal chandeliers and a grand staircase with intricate wrought-iron railings. One look at the expansive marble floor gave her the most wicked desire to slip on a pair of Rollerblades and race through the building, shouting "Cowabunga" at the top of her lungs.

She pressed the button beside the door, but Blake already knew who was there because security at the front gate had called to announce her.

"I'm glad to see you," he said after opening up.

"Hi." She wheeled her small weekend bag into the marble foyer, which mirrored the elegance of the building's lobby.

He frowned at her luggage. "Where's the rest of your bags?"

"We agreed to a trial basis. If it doesn't work out, why waste time and energy moving a lot of stuff?"

"So much for the power of positive thinking."

Casey used to be an optimist, but not anymore. "Never test the depth of the water with both feet."

"Right." He picked up her suitcase. "I guess you want to see where you'll be staying."

"Okay." She couldn't help noticing how wide his shoulders were as she followed. Nice butt, too. "Where's Mia?"

"In her room." He glanced back. "Doing homework."

"She's in summer school." It wasn't a question. Casey was taking classes, too, trying to finish up her degree as quickly as possible.

"I met with a school counselor, who recommended it. To keep her busy and out of trouble. Albeit without much success. Also, because her educational background is a little sketchy, what with her unstable upbringing. They want to see where she is academically before the term starts in September."

"A good idea."

She followed him past a living room with light green walls and wide crown molding and furnished with several love seats and a couple of chairs arranged in a grouping designed to facilitate conversation. Next was the kitchen-family room combination. There was a built-in cherrywood entertainment center with a plasma TV almost large enough for a movie theater. An L-shaped, overstuffed couch sat in front of it. The floor-to-ceiling windows offered an expansive view of the Las Vegas Valley, including a golf course and several hotel-casino resorts nearby.

As they continued walking past rooms, Casey admired the penthouse's understated elegance, cloud-soft carpet and recessed lighting, which showed off every detail to perfection.

"How big is this place?" she asked.

"Six thousand square feet, not counting the terrace." He looked down at her and grinned. "Give or take a square foot or two."

"Do you provide a GPS unit to your employees?"

"If you're as smart as Ginger Davis says, you'll learn your way around in no time." He walked into a room at the farthest corner of the penthouse. "Welcome to your new home, sweet home. I think you'll be comfortable."

She looked around at the oak armoire and matching dresser with a multitude of drawers, large and small. A floral comforter and a plethora of pink, green and maroon throw pillows covered the bed. To the right was a dressing area with a walk-in closet and a bathroom, which technically made this a suite. Chalk up one for her boss, the divorce lawyer.

"What do you think?"

She nodded. "It'll do."

"Good." He set her single suitcase on the tufted bench at the end of the bed. "It won't take you long to unpack. So, if you don't mind, I'd like to talk to you. In my study."

"Okay."

They retraced their steps, and somewhere beyond the family room, he turned right and entered another room. The desk, computer, and built-in bookcases holding big, fat, boring-looking books clued her in to the fact that this must be his study. Looked like an office to her, but when you had enough money, it probably earned you the right to call it whatever you wanted.

"Have a seat," he said, indicating the two leather barrel-shaped chairs in front of the desk.

Casey picked the one on the right and sat. "First of all, you should know that I need two evenings a week off and an afternoon on the weekend."

"How about *one* weeknight?" He was still standing on

the other side of the desk. Maybe he was striking an intimidating pose.

The thought almost made Casey smile. A five-star general
in the United States Army was intimidating. Blake Decker?
Not so much. As long as she ignored the gleam of amusement
in his blue eyes. Or the smokin' hot jawline, which could have
been carved out of a rugged peak in Red Rock Canyon. He
was wearing khaki shorts, a black T-shirt that highlighted
impressive muscles in his chest and arms, and flip-flops that
might have made him look like the dork Mia had accused him
of being. But the kid would be way wrong.

Casey refused to be intimidated. All he had to do was give
her even the ghost of a reason and she'd be so out of there.

She cleared her throat and didn't like the fact that to meet
his gaze, her chin rose slightly. It made her look defiant
instead of cool. And she so wanted to look cool. Frosty. Emotionally unengaged.

"I need two evenings off," she said. "I'm taking night
classes. It's not negotiable."

"That's a challenge, since negotiating is what I do."

His slow, challenging grin actually made her world tilt,
along with producing a shimmy and shake in her stomach.
The reaction was a big, honkin' clue that she should exercise
her escape clause and, well, escape.

"Look, Mr. Decker—"

"I asked you to call me Blake. Remember?"

And how. "Obviously you're good at what you do and it
pays pretty well, or you wouldn't live in the Parthenon."

"Excuse me?" If anything, the gleam in his eyes intensified.

"This complex is like a Greek temple with fountains, arch-
ways, anatomically correct sculptures and Roman columns."

"You're mixing your civilizations," he pointed out.

"And you're splitting hairs to distract me," she countered.

"I've been working my tail off to get a teaching credential and I'm almost there. Two evenings a week for classes, and either a Saturday or Sunday afternoon, your choice which. Those are my terms. Take it or leave it."

When she started to stand, he held his palms out in a conciliatory gesture.

"Yes, ma'am. Understood." He saluted, then sat in the plush desk chair. "Your military is showing."

Casey pressed fingertips to her chest and the scars hidden beneath her sleeveless cotton blouse, souvenirs of her time in the army. They were both a warning and a reminder that trusting anyone was a dangerous proposition. She'd let the wrong person come close, and an IED—an improvised explosive device—had taken her best friend's life and left her two little kids motherless. Blake Decker had no idea how much military she would always carry around with her.

"Another thing," she said, ignoring his charm. The man had buckets of charm and her military training hadn't prepared her for that. The army was about discipline, chain of command, following orders. There was no handbook for how to remain impassive when you were attracted to the person giving the orders. You were simply expected to follow the command without question.

"Yes?"

"From what you told me about Mia's background and the behavior I observed—"

"What a nice way to say she's a shoplifter."

"You can only be grateful that she's not very good at it."

"That already occurred to me," he admitted.

"I've been thinking about it, and in my opinion the two of you could benefit from counseling. I can give you several recommendations of excellent family therapists—"

"No."

She stared at him for a moment. "Just like that?"

"Yes."

"But negotiating is what you do," she reminded him.

"It is. But some things aren't worth a compromise. And going toe-to-toe with a Dr. Phil wannabe is one of them."

Casey recognized the heat of anger in his cool blue eyes and wondered about the nerve she'd stumbled on. "Mia would get a lot out of talking to someone."

"Talk is cheap."

"Not at the prices they charge," she pointed out.

"It's not the cost I object to." But he stopped short of saying what he *did* have a problem with in regard to seeing a counselor. "You get two out of three, Casey. Two evenings and an afternoon off. Any of my social engagements can be scheduled around your commitments."

"You mean dates?" The words popped out before she even realized the thought had formed.

"Yes," he confirmed.

"Are you dating anyone?" She really hoped she hadn't said that out loud, but the way his mouth curved up told her she wasn't that lucky. That was twice in a matter of seconds that the words were out before going through a rational thought process. It wasn't something she wanted to make a habit of.

"The only steady woman in my life besides my mother and Mia is an ex-wife I'd rather forget about."

Her not-so-stealthy recon had produced interesting results. He'd been married. He wasn't now. And there was no permanent arm candy.

The fact was, that information made her want to smile, a big clue that taking this assignment was a very bad idea.

"And," he added, "I'm not in the market for a romantic relationship."

"That makes two of us."

His eyebrows rose slightly, the only indication that her agreement surprised him. She had good reason for feeling that way. A person needed to trust to be able to form intimate ties and Blake seemed to be lacking in that department. It was something they had in common. A bomb in Iraq had blown her trust to kingdom come, which meant she wouldn't be forming ties anytime soon, either.

A week later, Blake stared at the stack of completed paperwork on his desk and figured productivity was the happy by-product of having his habitat invaded by females. His new norm was barricading himself in his study, instead of sitting on the couch in front of the TV to watch sports or the news or engage in other mindless entertainment.

Not that he wasn't using his mental capacity for other things.

One of the reasons he was cutting himself off from the invading females was that Casey had invaded his mind as well as his environment. He stared at the two chairs on the other side of his desk. A week ago she'd sat there and teased him about the way wealthy people lived. Instead of taking offense, he'd been impressed by her sense of humor. She was smart. Still, he knew a lot of smart women and spent little or no time thinking about them.

And flirty ones activated his gold-digger sensors. Casey wasn't flirty. Just the opposite.

She was clear that she wasn't interested in anything but a boss-employee relationship. Period. That one intrigued him.

He'd done love once, and the end had been painful and ugly. As a divorce attorney, a successful one, he spent every day representing clients who were looking to end painful and ugly relationships. That made him cautious and determined *not* to open that door again.

But what was Casey's story? What had happened to turn her off to romance?

A soft knock on the study door pulled his thoughts back to the moment. "Come in," he said.

Casey stood in the doorway. "Dinner's ready."

No salutation, small talk or frivolous chatter. She was straightforward and to the point. The devil of it was that she couldn't be further from his type. Her white cotton capris and black sleeveless top were a far cry from the silk and sequins his dates wore. Casey Thomas was all button-down efficiency and he couldn't stop thinking about *unbuttoning* her. How stupid was that?

He was her employer and an attorney. Any move in that direction on his part would be inappropriate, not to mention it would open the door for a sexual-harassment lawsuit.

"Blake?"

He met her gaze. "Hmm?"

"I said dinner's ready. I'm going to get Mia."

His niece. The whole reason Casey was here. And since he'd hired her, there hadn't been a single phone call from the school or the police. That made him cautiously optimistic that the new nanny was the solution to the Mia problem. Another excellent reason to continue keeping his distance.

"You and Mia go ahead and eat without me. I have a lot of work to do."

Instead of backing out of the room, as she'd done every other evening, she advanced on him, and the look in her eyes could best be described as determined.

"We need to talk."

Four words a man never wanted to hear coming out of a woman's mouth. Especially when the mouth in question was as kissable as Casey's. There were about a million things he would rather do with it that didn't include conversation.

"We'll schedule a meeting. "I've got to get through this stack by tomorrow—"

"You're here. I'm here. By my definition it's a meeting." She sat down in one of the chairs across from him. "And what I have to say won't take long."

Definitely determined.

"I'm not going to beat around the bush."

He'd have been surprised if she did. "What's on your mind?" he asked.

"Work is not an acceptable excuse for avoidance."

She knew he was dodging her? Offense was always the best defense. "Six thousand square feet of high-end real estate doesn't come cheap. It takes billable hours. Keyword *hours*. I have to put in a lot of them to pay the rent."

"It's not about a roof over your head," she shot back. "This behavior appears to run in the family. Mia has inherited the evasion gene, too."

"What are you talking about?"

"She's hiding in her room, the same way you are here in your study."

"I'm glad to hear she's hitting the books," he said, trying to deflect some of the truth.

"How do you know that's what she's doing?"

"If she's in there, what else would she be up to?"

Her wry, pitying look was a clue that his remark was going to bite him in the backside. "She has a computer with Internet access, a cell phone, a house line and a TV. Those are the most obvious electronic devices. And this is a girl who everyone, including herself, admits has had a rocky go of things so far."

"And your point?"

"Do you seriously believe that a couple of weeks in your high-end real estate has turned her into a disciplined scholar focused on good grades and college goals?"

When she put it like that, he didn't. The truth was, he hadn't given Mia a lot of thought at all. Everything with his niece seemed to be under control. Casey was the one he'd spent too much time thinking about.

"You're saying she has distractions," he said.

"Yes."

"So tell me how dinner is going to change things. Especially a dinner with me there."

"A meal together isn't just nourishment for the body. It goes a long way toward feeding the soul."

He tilted his head and studied her serious expression. "Do you really believe that?"

"Completely."

"Why?"

"Your niece needs to feel stable and secure. A family unit around a dinner table is the best place to start."

"Why?" he said again.

"It shows you care."

"Right." He and his ex-wife, Debra, had eaten together a lot, and he'd found out how much she cared when he caught her in bed with his best friend. "Look, Casey, I appreciate your dedication above and beyond the call of duty, but—"

"That's not all," she interrupted. "It's an opportunity for you to find out what's going on with her."

He leaned forward and rested his forearms on the desk. "Just to be clear and make sure we're on the same page, you are talking about Mia Decker, my niece?"

"Yes."

"The same one whose default response is, 'Whatever'? The girl who thinks I'm the dork who's trying to dump her? That's the kid you're talking about?"

"Hostility is a defense mechanism."

"It's effective." He knew a thing or two about hostility.

"The thing is that if you show up and she gets used to you being there, eventually she'll start talking. Whether she means to or not, she'll give you clues about what's going on in her life, good and bad. But communication isn't all about talking. Listening is an important component. You can't do that if you're isolated in this room. For whatever reason."

His gaze snapped to hers. "So for Mia it's a defense mechanism, and I'm a head case?"

"That's not what I said—"

It was implied. "Look, Casey, you're a soldier slash nanny whose primary responsibility is being my niece's bodyguard."

"Blake, I—"

He held up his hand. "The point is that it's not your job to get into my head. Others have tried and failed."

"That's not what I'm doing." Anger flashed in her eyes as she scooted to the edge of her seat. "Mia has been neglected and left to fend for herself. An expensive roof over her head doesn't mean it's not still happening."

"I repeat, you were hired to keep her safe."

"I'm paid to do that, but you're her biological family. She tries to hide it, but like every other human being on the planet, she's looking for love and acceptance. The more you keep her at arm's length, the more you reinforce that she's not lovable. Blake, you have to—"

He held up a finger to silence her. "Don't tell me what I have to do. She has a place to live. It's your job to tell me what she needs—food, clothes, school supplies. It's my job to write the check."

Anger and something that looked a lot like disapproval swirled in her eyes, making the gold and green flecks that turned to hazel a lot darker. It was almost as if he could see the wheels in her head turning, words pressing to get out. Finally she stood and all but saluted when she snapped out a curt, "Yes, sir."

And then he was alone.

It should have been a relief, but it definitely wasn't. Verbal sparring with Casey was the most invigorating thing he'd done in a very long time. He should be mad as hell. In any other employee he'd call it impertinence. But her earnestness had come through loud and clear, erasing any hint of insolence. He believed she was genuinely trying to help, but he didn't need it. Mia was far better off than she'd ever been in her life and didn't need him meddling.

He'd made a mess of his own life. Who was he to tell Mia what to do? That was for the nanny. The one with a mouth made for kissing. And a body with curves in all the right places.

The one he couldn't stop thinking about.

And he wondered, not for the first time, if hiring Casey was as good in reality as it had looked on paper.

Chapter Three

"Boring."

Casey glanced over at Mia, who was slouched in the front passenger seat of her Corolla. They'd just sat through a college class on Shakespeare's tragedies, and as tragic as the girl looked, it was quite possible she'd actually absorbed something.

"I'm shocked and appalled that studying Shakespeare doesn't make you do the happy dance."

The girl responded with a dramatic eye roll. Casey wished she'd had the luxury of sinking to that level when she confronted her boss about not showing up as agreed so that she could attend class without having to bring Mia along. Blake Decker could have been a bigger ass, but she wasn't sure how. Actually, that wasn't true. He was a bigger jerk when he'd told her his only responsibility to his niece was paying the bills.

Casey glanced over at Mia. "If I'm being honest, and I

always try, Shakespeare doesn't excite me much, either. But it's something I need for my degree and I've put it off as long as I can."

"You didn't have to drag me along with you. I don't need a babysitter. I can take care of myself."

Three whole sentences, Casey thought. *Must be a record. Or the kid is really ticked off.* "At least you had something to read."

Mia looked out the window at the Suncoast Hotel marquee as they turned right onto Alta Avenue.

"Is it a book you're reading for school?" Casey asked, trying to keep her talking.

"No."

"Wow. Reading for fun. What a concept."

No verbal response. The only answer was a shoulder lift.

"So," Casey said, "what's the book about? And before you shrug, sigh or roll your eyes, remember the polite thing would be to use words."

Mia glared. "It's some stupid teenage vampire romance trash."

"Hmm." Casey turned the car into the driveway leading to the One Queensridge Place complex and the guard waved as she drove by. "It looked to me like you're at least halfway through a book that's five or six hundred pages long. I'm going to guess that you didn't get that far into it during my hour-long class, so you've been at it awhile. Good for you. How did you pick it?"

"Some girls mentioned it."

"So you're making friends?" Casey asked.

"No. I heard them talking."

"Are you reaching out to the girls at school?"

"What's the point?" Mia looked at her as if she were as dumb as a rock. "I won't be there that long."

"Why not? You have a home now, Mia. It's okay to relax and put down roots. Make friends."

"He's going to dump me."

Her uncle. The same one taking jerk status to new and even lower levels. "That's not what he told me." This is where verbal acuity came in handy for creating spin. Casey parked the car and turned off the engine. "He said you'd always have a place to live." A slight exaggeration of that infuriating conversation.

"Right." Sarcasm was thick in Mia's voice. "Wow. I guess I should worship at the altar of Saint Uncle Blake. Except where was he when my mom needed help? Where were her parents?"

"Your grandparents," Casey said, putting a finer point on it. "Without knowing the facts, it's hard to comment on your family—"

"They're not my family. Families are supposed to be there for each other. These people weren't."

Casey wanted to sigh, glare, roll her eyes or lift a shoulder in reply, because she didn't know what to say to that. In a perfect world family *would* be a support system. But after her own mother died, her father had withdrawn from her. It had been like losing both parents at the same time.

"Family dynamics are complicated, Mia. Your uncle made it clear that you're to have whatever you need. Money is no object." That was the best way to spin what he'd said about it being her job to make the list and he'd write the check.

"Don't go Mary Poppins on me. You see what he's like. You had a deal with him. He was supposed to be home and take over, but he hung you out to dry. Mom said her family didn't want her. You do the math."

Before Casey could think of something reassuring, your basic lie, the girl was out of the car and walking toward the private elevator. Just as well, because Casey hated lies and she couldn't think of anything else to say. She used her key card to access the top floor and they rode up in silence.

Inside the penthouse Mia disappeared down the hall, and

her disappearance was followed closely by the sound of a door closing. Forcefully.

Anger that had simmered when Blake was a no-show earlier now came to a full boil. Casey tracked him down in the kitchen, where he was making a sandwich, and it looked like he hadn't been there long. The matching suit coat to the charcoal slacks was missing, but he was still wearing his wrinkled white dress shirt, with the sleeves rolled to mid-forearm. The gray-on-black silk tie was loosened, and the first shirt button undone. His dark hair was stylishly tousled or he'd run his fingers through it a lot. Either way, the look worked far too well and was a major distraction when she wanted to be nothing but furious.

She set her notebook and purse on the granite-topped island in the center of the room. "I see you're no longer missing in action."

"I knew where I was the whole time." The words were full of charm and might have distracted her if she weren't so angry.

"You know what I mean."

"This was the night of your class. My secretary said she relayed the message that I'd be late."

"You agreed to my terms," Casey challenged. "One of which was two nights a week you'd be here so I could go to my class."

"Something came up."

"Not good enough, Counselor."

His eyes widened and he set the sandwich on the white plate. He picked up the longneck bottle of beer beside it and took a drink. "It's all I've got. When the judge says, 'Be in court,' I show up."

"No one else in your office could have gone instead?"

A flicker in his eyes said the challenge hit the mark. "I told you up front that my hours are unpredictable. That's why I've got you."

"You did tell me that," she agreed. "But my schedule is predictable and you approved the arrangement to be here on specific days. You weren't here as promised, which means you broke your word."

"I apologize. Clearly you worked it out."

She waited, but he didn't add that it wouldn't happen again. Folding her arms over her chest, she rested a hip against the island as she stared across the expanse at her boss. He was as extraordinarily stubborn as he was handsome and that was saying a lot about the stubborn part.

"You know, the first rule of parenting is to do what you say," she said.

"Okay." He finished half his sandwich and wiped his mouth with a napkin that he'd grabbed from the chrome holder on the counter. "Is there more?"

"If consequences are clearly defined, when a kid decides to break a rule, there should be no surprises when punishment is swift and sure."

"Is there a point to this parenting protocols lecture?"

The gleam in his blue eyes sent a tsunami-sized tremble rolling through her, and something that big could never be good, but she took a deep breath and dove in. "I took this job on a trial basis."

"And I have to say that your work is exemplary. Mia is under control and your conscientious attention to detail is clearly getting results."

"You're the one on probation, Blake. And I have to tell you, I don't like what I'm seeing."

"Excuse me?" He took another sip of beer. "You're saying that I don't meet your standards?"

"Pretty much. I'd planned to take time off while getting these classes out of the way, but I agreed to work for you as a favor to Ginger. Now I see it was a mistake."

"Are you quitting?" he asked.

For a moment he wasn't a wealthy, confident, high-powered attorney, but a man without a clue about dealing with a preteen girl. She could also see that he didn't like not being in complete control. It was a characteristic shared by a lot of military men. But this wasn't the military and she could walk away without consequences.

Considering the way he affected her, that would be the smartest move. "Give me one good reason why I shouldn't resign."

"Mia needs you."

"She needs a family. That's you."

"I'm here."

"No. Your checkbook is here. You're in court. Or your office. Or the study here at home. Or wherever else you can find to avoid her." Casey drew in a deep breath. "She's asking questions, Blake. And I don't have the answers for her."

"What kind of questions?"

"Like where you and your parents were when her mother was in bad shape."

Casey wouldn't be human if she wasn't curious about that, too. But she didn't ask and he didn't volunteer.

"It wasn't the Decker family's finest hour," he admitted.

She held up her hands. "I don't need to know. I'm just saying that Mia does. She's bitter and angry."

"Isn't that a teenager's stock-in-trade?" One corner of his mouth curved up but the teasing comment did nothing to clear the shadows in his eyes.

"This is more than that." She traced the circular beige pattern in the granite countertop for a moment. "She's scared, confused and mad as hell. I say again, on the record, counseling could help with that."

"Is it a condition for getting you to stay?"

That was a nonanswer if she'd ever heard one. Which

made him a good attorney, but it wasn't especially helpful in figuring out why he was so resistive. One look around his pricey, spacious penthouse made it clear that money wasn't the problem. And he'd all but admitted screwing up with his sister, but she was the last person to judge anyone's past. In Iraq people had counted on her and she'd let them down. It felt pretty crappy. She wasn't about to do that to a kid who'd been let down enough in her very short life.

"No," she finally said. "It's not a condition for me to stay."

Now he did smile, a full-on, take-no-prisoners grin that made the hair at her nape prickle, signaling danger as surely as if she were on patrol in downtown Baghdad. What the hell? She used to be a soldier. Yeah, there were a lot of women in the military now, but she'd spent the majority of her time with men. Not once had she felt this way. Personal relationships had been discouraged and for good reason. They were a distraction none of them could afford in a war zone.

Somehow One Queensridge Place had turned into a theater of conflict, one that had nothing to do with rocket propelled grenades, IEDs, bombs or body armor. If only she could put on a bullet-proof vest to protect herself from whatever it was that she was feeling for Blake Decker, because it smacked of improper. Technically, she couldn't actually control it, and impropriety would only happen if she acted on it. That wasn't an option, mainly because she was already carrying around more than her fair share of guilt.

Blake took a sip of his beer, and the act was so incredibly masculine that it violated the spirit of conviction she'd had just moments before.

He looked at her, and the confident, charming gleam in his eyes was turned on full blast. "So, can I take that as a yes? You'll stick around and extend my period of probation? I promise not to let you down again."

If only that were true. Mia's words were still too fresh in her mind. He hung her out to dry. If Casey was smart, she'd retreat right now. But Mia didn't have anyone else in her corner.

"Yes, I'll stay."

Blake hit the down button on the TV remote's channel selector, wishing desperately for football season to start, but it was only the end of July. In a few more weeks the exhibition games would start, but not today. Today he still felt like a prisoner in his own home. Like he had a guest who would never leave and a second in command who'd deserted a sinking ship. And he was on probation, which meant he was here alone with Mia while Casey had the afternoon off.

Facing twelve jurors was less intimidating than dealing with a disgruntled twelve-year-old. Not that he'd seen her, because his niece had been in her room for hours. Should he go check on her? Was that a breach of privacy? How much privacy did a girl need, anyway? If Casey were here, he could ask her, but she wasn't.

At least she was coming back—soon he hoped. He'd nearly blown it with her. Calling her bluff on the terms of her time off wasn't his brightest move, and he wasn't even sure why he'd pushed the envelope. He could have gotten home in time for her to get to class without taking Mia. Maybe he'd wanted to show her who was in command. It might have been his way of pushing back against her dictating the terms of employment. He was used to coming and going without thinking about anyone but himself—and that was the way he liked it.

What he didn't like was the curve fate had thrown him. Karma was probably having a good laugh at his expense, what with making him responsible for a kid—a girl, no less. That was bad enough, but he'd gotten a glimpse of what it would be like to raise the kid without backup, a sneak peek of him and Mia without a referee. It hadn't been pretty.

Blake had hired Casey with every intention of dumping all the responsibility for his niece in her lap. She'd surprised him by pushing back, giving him things to think about, which he didn't much like. He could probably find another nanny but he wasn't keen on starting the process again. And no matter how hard he tried, he couldn't manage to forget what Casey had said about Mia needing a family. Although, with his legendary power of selective memory, he'd managed to put her pitch for counseling out of his mind. It hadn't worked for him and Debra. It hadn't prevented her cheating, which doomed their relationship.

This penthouse used to be his sanctuary; now there was a twelve-year-old stranger here. Should he go in and talk to her? Did he really want to bring up the past? Wasn't it enough that he'd given her a nice place to live and three square meals a day? Didn't he get sufficient points for taking her in?

"You look deep in thought." Casey stood in the family room doorway.

Blake was so glad to see her that he felt the most absurd urge to kiss her. Not actually that absurd, since his thoughts went there a lot. At the moment he also felt the burden that had been weighing him down just moments before suddenly lift.

"Hi." He hit the power button to turn off the TV.

"Hi." She lifted a hand in greeting. "I just wanted to let you know I'm back. I'll just go see—"

"Wait," he said.

"Is everything all right? Mia?"

"She's fine."

"Where is she?"

"In her room. Doing homework." That part was just a guess, but what else would she be doing in there all this time?

Casey tucked a strand of straight blond hair behind her ear. "Was there something you wanted?"

"Just wondering how your afternoon off was," he said, slipping his fingertips into the pockets of his khaki shorts.

"Fine."

While waiting for her to say more, he moved across the expansive room, suddenly needing to shrink the distance between them. When she didn't elaborate, he asked, "What did you do?"

"Does it matter?"

"Not unless you're moonlighting at a topless gentlemen's club," he teased. "I'm quite sure it says something in the parenting handbook about that not being a positive influence on a preteen girl."

As hoped for, Casey laughed. "No pole dancing for me, you'll be relieved to know. Just a visit home. Sunday family dinner with my father and three brothers."

"Three brothers?"

She nodded. "The youngest one is Bradley, named after the fighting vehicle. Middle brother is Colin, which came from General Colin Powell. And Norm—"

"Don't tell me. General Schwartzkopf?"

"That's the one." She laughed.

"I sense a theme. Where did the name Casey come from?"

"I'm not sure." She shrugged.

"Obviously the inspiration in naming your brothers came from the military. Didn't you ever ask?"

"I was too busy trying to figure out where I fit in the all male environment."

"I can't help noticing you didn't mention your mother," Blake said.

"She died when I was about Mia's age."

"I'm sorry." His parents wouldn't win any awards, but at

least he had them. He couldn't imagine what she, or Mia, for that matter, had gone through.

"It was a long time ago." Casey shrugged. "I'm all grown up now."

He'd definitely noticed that. Her denim capris and sleeveless white cotton shirt were not especially sexy, except that she was wearing them. And every time he was this close to her, heat was an issue. It was July and hot enough to cook an egg on the sidewalk, but that didn't explain his acute reaction to the nanny.

"Obviously you missed your mother," Blake said.

"Why obviously?"

"Just an impression, I guess. What you said about fitting into an all-male world."

She pressed her lips together for a moment as shadows flitted through her eyes. "It's not easy for a girl to grow up without a female around."

"Did that factor into your decision to accept this job? Or was it completely a favor to Ginger?"

One slender shoulder lifted in a careless movement, but the intensity in her expression was anything but casual. "Mia's background, the loss of her mother, I'll admit that had something to do with my decision."

"Is your father a military man?"

"What was your first clue?"

"You mean besides naming your youngest brother after a tank?"

"Yeah."

Her mouth curved up at the corners and amusement made her eyes sparkle. It would be so easy to forget she was the nanny, but if he did, he'd be at the mercy of his testosterone. That would make him ready, willing and able to act on the impulse to explore his fascination for her contradictions. She was, after all, the most feminine soldier he could imagine.

"My dad was a career army man," she admitted. "He is retired now and works in engineering and maintenance at the Bellagio hotel."

"Did your brothers all serve in the military?"

She shook her head. "None of them joined up."

That was a surprise. "And you did? The only girl in the group?"

"Go figure."

"It's hard for me to imagine you in camouflage, carrying a rifle." He shrugged. "Call me a sexist pig—"

"You're a sexist pig."

The words were teasing, but the shadows were back in her eyes, and he kicked himself for putting them there. She had peddled the benefits of counseling to him more than once, but a shrink would have a field day with her.

"Seriously, Casey, what made you join the army?"

"What made you want to be a lawyer?" she shot back.

Whoa. That had touched a nerve. "I'm sorry. I didn't mean to pry. Military men and women sacrifice a lot to keep this country safe, and I'd never belittle that. You're a natural with Mia and it seems a contradiction—"

"I don't want to talk about it."

Her tension was visible and he wondered what was troubling her. She hadn't reacted this way when she'd mentioned the family dinner, and she'd seemed sincere when she said her mother's passing wasn't a current tragedy. By a process of elimination, he realized it was his inquiries about the military that had triggered this reaction.

"I didn't mean to offend you. But now that I have, maybe talking about whatever's bothering you might help. You're the counseling queen—"

"Don't knock it till you've tried it."

"Have you?"

"What if I have?"

Not an answer, he noticed. At best it was an evasive maneuver. *Your Honor, permission to treat this witness as hostile.* That wasn't exactly the right word. *Wounded* was the one that popped into his mind when he stared into her big hazel eyes. He remembered thinking after knowing her for less than an hour that she had the sexiest mouth this side of heaven and the saddest eyes he'd ever seen. Something had happened to her when she was in the army. He'd bet his very successful law practice on it.

"If you have had counseling," he said, "I mean, I'd advise you to get your money back, because there are clearly some unresolved issues that need dealing with. I'm not especially insightful, but I am pretty fluent in body language, and yours says that you'd rather have dental implants without Novocain than talk about this."

Full-blown distress was apparent in her expression, and she looked ready to cut and run. It was his fault. In his own defense, he wasn't used to a woman's wounded looks. His ex had looked alternately angry and frustrated when he didn't drop everything in the universe for a broken fingernail. Just before everything hit the fan, she'd simply looked bored.

And then she'd taken up with his best friend. Also an ex. One ex plus one ex equals two exes, algebraically speaking.

But this wasn't about him. He was trying to help Casey and he had the most insane desire to pull her into his arms. He reached out his hand and curved his fingers around her upper arm, simply to touch her and offer comfort for the as yet un-talked-about something making her look as if she'd lost her only friend.

Her skin was soft and silky and warm. She felt delicate, so very vulnerable, and again he had trouble seeing her as a combat soldier. She was a woman, a desirable woman. A really desirable woman who looked in desperate need of a hug.

Blake stared into her eyes as his pulse rate continued to head upward, and in the next moment he was pulling her against him. "Casey—"

Her eyes widened and she backed away from him as surprise pushed the sadness from her eyes. "I have to go check on Mia."

"Of course. Yeah. Right." He curled his fingers into his palm. "That's a good idea."

In a nanosecond she was gone, and he walked over to the floor-to-ceiling windows and a spectacular view of the setting sun. The gold, orange, pink and purple in the sky were Mother Nature's palette and a fitting backdrop against which to kick himself for what he'd almost done.

Casey was his employee and he owed her nothing but a paycheck. If she had personal problems, she had a support system to lean on. Ginger. Her father and brothers. Probably girlfriends. Even if it was about man trouble, something that didn't set well with him, it was still none of his business. In the reflection in the windows, he saw Casey walk back into the room.

"Where's Mia?" she asked.

He turned. "I already told you she's in her room."

"I just looked. She's not there. When did you last see her?"

He'd seen her at breakfast and when Casey had said goodbye. "After you left, I was in the study working for a few hours."

"What about after that?"

"I've been in here watching TV ever since," he hedged.

"So you didn't check on her at all?"

When she put it like that, he felt like the biggest jerk on the planet. Especially because he'd been relieved that his niece hadn't demanded his time. "I figured she was studying."

"For six hours?" She shook her head, and the pitying expression was back, laced with worry. "Obviously she sneaked out and there's no telling how long ago. We have to look for her."

"There's a mall not too far away," he offered. "Boca Park is pretty upscale. She might have gone there."

"We have to start somewhere. She told me she's not bothering to make friends at school, because it's a waste of time since you're only going to dump her."

If that remark was meant to make him feel guilty, it came dangerously close to being successful. Before he could grab his keys, the phone rang and he picked up the extension in the kitchen. "Hello?"

"Blake?"

"Hi, Dad."

"Mia is at the door and your mother is furious. This is not how it was supposed to go."

"I'm on my way."

Blake was used to drama, but it mostly happened in his office. His last thought before dashing out the door was one of gratitude that he had Casey in his corner.

Chapter Four

Casey sat in the front passenger seat of Blake's Mercedes sedan. She was unaccustomed to being surrounded by luxury, and the softness of the leather surprised her. She wished Mia's unpredictability surprised her, too, but it didn't. Even if Blake hadn't clued her in right after they'd met, she'd seen it for herself the first time Mia took off and disappeared at the Fashion Show Mall.

Now that she knew the girl was safe, relatively speaking—a pun, considering she'd turned up with her grandparents—Casey could admit to herself that the disappearing act was a relief. It took the heat off her.

Blake's cross-examination about her family background had stirred up memories that she'd rather not revisit. He'd gotten on every nerve she had. In all fairness he hadn't touched on what had happened in Iraq, but only because he didn't know about it. And he never would, because it was one more thing she'd rather leave alone.

What she needed to deal with was her current predicament. She didn't want to care about another kid who would let her down, another child who was playing her. And Mia's behavior tonight was cause for concern. When she'd seen the empty room and realized the girl was gone, fear had immediately set in. That didn't happen when her feelings were idling in neutral.

And speaking of neutral, it hadn't escaped her notice that Blake had planned to kiss her. If only she could have been disinterested, but she'd been far *too* interested. Stepping away from him had taken discipline, and she wasn't sure where it had come from or whether she could manage to find it again. Should the need arise, which she prayed didn't happen.

"We're almost there," Blake said, slowing as he steered the car through a set of open guard gates.

His voice pulled her away from the disturbing thoughts and she studied the large entrance. "King Kong gates," she commented.

"Excuse me?"

"Didn't you ever see the nineteen thirties movie with Fay Wray? The big ape looks over this gate like it's a speed bump. Those big iron gates into the neighborhood remind me of that—tall and strong to keep out the big, hairy riffraff."

He laughed. "I have to face the folks and deal with Mia fallout. Under the circumstances I didn't think anyone could make me laugh. Thanks for coming along, Casey."

"You're welcome." Then his words sank in. "Mia fallout? What does that mean?"

Without answering, he pulled up in front of an imposing house with impressive columns in front. "Showtime."

"This looks like Tara," she said, studying the grand house.

"Another movie reference?"

She nodded. *"Gone with the Wind."*

"A Civil War reference." He looked at her. "You're about to find out how appropriate that is."

Just what Casey needed—another war zone. Not. But Mia was clearly feeling the effects of being ignored, and it was understandable. Casey was ready to roll and go to the kid's defense.

She followed Blake into the house. He didn't knock and the front door was unlocked.

They heard voices and Blake said, "They're in the sitting room."

"Because Tara doesn't have a family room," she muttered.

It turned out that the room was right off the entryway and had a fireplace, as well as two hunter green floral love seats facing each other at a right angle to it. A big coffee table and two wing chairs completed the conversation area, but no one was sitting there. Although there was talking, right now Mia was doing most of it.

Blake's father was a handsome, tall, silver-haired man, a preview of what his son would look like in his later years. A brunette, his mother was in her sixties and was still beautiful. Casey had seen shell shock and knew the older woman was feeling it now.

"My mother was pregnant," Mia shouted. "You guys threw her away like a piece of trash. Over a baby. It's not a crime to have a baby."

"Blake. Thank God you're here," his mother said.

"What in the blazes is going on?" his father demanded. He looked at Casey. "Who are you?"

"Casey Thomas." She walked up to him with her hand extended and he shook it.

"Lincoln Decker," he said. "My wife, Patricia."

Casey shook the woman's hand and, before Blake's parents could ask, said, "I'm your granddaughter's nanny."

"This hooligan?" Lincoln said. "She barged in unannounced and has been accusing us of atrocities ever since."

"Why don't we all sit?" Blake suggested. "We can get acquainted."

"Why?" the older man demanded.

"That goes double for me." Mia's comment was a clear indication that she was not taking responsibility for setting this scenario in motion.

"Blake, you've hired a nanny. How long has Mia been with you?" his mother whispered.

"Not that long," Blake hedged.

"Long enough for you to hire a nanny, but not long enough for you to tell us about Mia?" Patricia's expression was accusatory.

"Dad knew," Blake said. "Children's services contacted him first."

"And you didn't tell me about her?" Patricia turned the heat of her expression on her husband.

"I was protecting you," Lincoln said.

"From what?" Patricia demanded.

"That would be me," Mia interjected. "Delinquent in training."

The conversation deteriorated from there. As an objective observer without an equal emotional investment, Casey watched the three adults and one child, who all were doing a lot of talking and very little listening. She couldn't help but notice the family resemblance. A glare here, an angry gesture there. Stubborn chin. The shape of the face. Even to the untrained eye, it was obvious that these people shared DNA, if not harmony. But they were getting nowhere fast.

Casey decided to play UN peacekeeping force. "Time-out," she said. When no one paid any attention to her, she whistled, a shrill sound that never failed to get her noticed. "Listen up. Everyone needs to sit down."

Lincoln stared, his displeasure obvious. "Just a moment—"

"Excuse me, sir, but I'm taking control."

"What gives you the right?" Lincoln demanded.

"Because I'm a calm, impartial spectator, and you've had a shock."

"I'm not a shock," Mia said, outraged.

"That's not what your grandmother said," Casey pointed out, shooting a questioning look at Blake.

"Mom, I was going to explain, but—"

"No buts," his mother said. "This is one of those situations that don't call for a but. You should have said something to me. Both of you. I had a right to know. Sooner or later I'd have to know. I can't believe she's been here and neither of you said a word to me—"

"Our daughter ran off and broke your heart," her husband said. "I was protecting you."

"Everyone please sit," Casey ordered, when the older woman started to protest.

Four pairs of eyes blinked at her and she stared them down until everyone found a seat. The elder Deckers sat side by side on a love seat, with Blake across from them. Mia was by herself on a wing chair that faced the fireplace.

"This situation could have been handled more diplomatically." Still standing, Casey gave Mia a look, but the girl wouldn't meet her gaze. "I think everyone needs to take a step back and let reality sink in."

"The reality is they're dorks," Mia said. "Old ones."

"I feel so special," Blake said sarcastically. "I fall into the young dork category."

"Not helping," Casey told him. "Be Switzerland."

"What?"

"Neutral," Casey explained. "After a cooling-off period, a mutually agreeable time for a mediation should be selected."

Lincoln looked at his son. "You took responsibility for her. That means you must not let her run wild. You have to control her, Blake."

"Right. Like you did with April," Blake shot back. "Or is this a 'do as I say, not as I do' situation?"

"Accusations are counterproductive," Casey said. "Until you can get along—"

"Not holding my breath," Mia mumbled.

Casey knew how it felt to be an outsider and sympathized with the kid. It was hard not taking her side, but that would most likely result in a resumption of hostilities. It would be detrimental to the peace process.

"Mia," Casey said in a firm, "listen up, or else" tone. "Please wait for us in the car."

"But—"

"As your grandmother said, no buts. That's an order. Orders are meant to be followed without discussion."

"This is sooo stupid."

"I think you need another *o* in there so we know how you really feel," Blake said.

Casey shook her head. "You're the adult. Focus. Mia?"

The girl glared for several moments, then presumably did as she'd been told—following a slam of the front door.

Lincoln stared after her for several moments, then looked at Casey. "Well done, young woman."

"Thank you, sir." *Not my job to judge these people, who are strangers,* Casey thought. But how could they fail to acknowledge the child of their child? All the facts were not in evidence, and that was for another time. "As I was saying, take a break. Talk again soon."

Lincoln nodded. "I like you, Casey. You've got spunk."

"You're very wise for one so young," Patricia said.

"Yeah, chalk one up for the young dorks," Blake muttered.

Casey looked at him and sighed. "I think it's time for us to go."

"You'll get no argument from me." Blake stood and walked to the doorway.

Casey said goodbye to the older couple and followed Blake out onto the front porch. She glanced at the Mercedes and saw Mia slouching against it, and relief flooded her that the girl hadn't taken off. This was the second time and Casey didn't trust her to stay put. Again, it was hard not to blame her when she'd had confirmation that her grandfather knew about her and didn't want her.

As they walked down the steps to the car, Blake said, "You really earned your paycheck tonight."

"I should get hazard pay for dealing with your family."

"Amen."

"So how did I earn my paycheck?" she asked, unable to stop the glow his praise was generating inside her.

"My dad approves of you. You've got spunk."

"Hoo-yah," she said.

Casey walked from Mia's bedroom, past her own and into the family room. She glanced outside and spotted Blake on the terrace, staring out at the carpet of light that was the Las Vegas Valley. He had a drink in his hand and she couldn't blame him. It had been a hell of a night. She was sorry if he wanted to be alone, but she was about to disturb his solitude.

After opening the slider, she went out, instantly feeling the desert heat mix with the cool air from inside. Because this was the top floor of the building, there was room for a pool, and the lights at the bottom illuminated the immediate surrounding area. There was also a fire pit, patio tables, chairs and chaise longues scattered around. It was surreal and magical.

Casey had the most absurd desire to pinch herself, as a reminder that she wasn't Dorothy, that this wasn't Kansas *or* Oz. She wasn't off to see the wizard, but she and Blake needed to talk.

"Mia's asleep."

"That was fast." He glanced over his shoulder.

"She's exhausted." It was warm outside, but considering the daytime temperature had topped out at over one hundred and ten, the breeze made the outside almost comfortable. "It takes a lot of energy to maintain that level of anger."

"And mobility." He drained the liquor in his glass and set it on a table. "Did she tell you how she managed to find her way to my parents?"

"She found out where they live from your address book on your computer. Then she took a cab."

"Do I want to know how she paid for it?"

"Your dad coughed up the fare."

His dark eyebrows rose in surprise. "Someone feels guilty."

"As well he should." Casey leaned her elbows on the metal railing that capped the clear glass separating luxury from certain death if one fell. "I know he's your dad and you love him, blah, blah. But I can't believe he knew about Mia and not only didn't make an effort to know her, but kept it all from your mom."

A sizzle of heat flashed through her when he rested his forearms beside hers and their shoulders brushed. "Any questions you may have regarding my dysfunctional tendencies should all be answered after meeting Lincoln and Patricia Decker."

"Some," she admitted, laughing. "But not all. I got the feeling your mother was a little peeved at him."

A ghost of a grin curved up the corners of his wonderful lips. "You're a quick study of human nature."

"Not really." And not when it counted the most. If she were, two little kids would still have their mom, and she'd have her best friend when she needed her most.

"You're right," he said. "Dad is in for a rough time. I'd say he'll be sleeping on the couch, but you saw the size of that place."

"Yeah. I'm guessing he'll have his choice of Tara's ten or twelve extra bedrooms when he's in the doghouse." Only a slight exaggeration.

"Give or take," he agreed. "Is there any chance that Mia didn't understand?"

"You mean the part where her grandfather didn't want to have anything to do with her, then kept it from his wife to protect the family?"

"Yeah, that."

"Nope. She understood perfectly."

"That pretty much sucks." The silver glow from a nearly full moon highlighted his frown and the tension in his shoulders.

"Yeah. Mia would like him put to sleep. That's a direct quote."

"That's a little harsh, although I can see where she's coming from."

Casey straightened and leaned a hip against the railing as she studied him. "Speaking of dysfunctional—"

"Uh-oh." He half turned toward her and met her gaze, folding his arms over his chest. "I'm not going to like this, am I?"

"You didn't the first two times I brought it up, but maybe the third time's the charm."

"Ever the optimist," he said dryly.

"Just call me the bluebird of happiness."

He laughed, then took a deep breath. "Okay. Get it over with."

"Counseling." The single word had tension running through him. She was close enough to feel it.

"Casey, we've been through this."

"I take it the third time is *not* the charm."

"And you're like a dog that won't let loose of a favorite bone."

"Because," she said, "I think it's important. You told me to make the list and you'd write the check. So on top of vitamins, a training bra and supplies for that time of the month—"

He started humming and covered his ears. "This is me not listening to that. And shame on you for mentioning it."

She laughed. It was such a guy reaction and said more about his feelings than even he realized. But this was serious and important. There was only one way she could think of to get him to listen and understand that she meant business.

She pushed his hands down. "You're hilarious."

"Thank you."

"It wasn't a compliment. Blake, I'm making counseling a condition of my continuing to be Mia's nanny."

If only she could give him an ultimatum about toning down his sex appeal, her life would be far less complicated.

He didn't look surprised. "Is that a card you really want to play?"

"It might be overstepping, but I feel very strongly about this, and I'm willing to take the risk."

"Really? I couldn't tell."

"Stop being charming—"

"You think I'm charming?"

"That's not the point."

He grinned a very self-satisfied male grin. "I'll take that as a yes."

"You're changing the subject." And she was blushing, which she desperately hoped he couldn't see. The heat wasn't only in her cheeks. It was everywhere, and her heart fluttered against the inside of her chest like a caged bird struggling for freedom. "I'm very serious about this."

"I don't have a lot of faith in counseling," he said seriously.

"Have you ever tried it?"

"What if I have?" he shot back, defiant and defensive in equal parts.

She remembered saying the same thing to him. Just because a few sessions with an army shrink hadn't squeegeed the guilt from her conscience didn't mean he and Mia wouldn't benefit from talking to someone. His presence alone could go a long way toward convincing the girl he cared. And one didn't need credentials to see she desperately wanted someone to care. Casey knew how that felt.

"Look, Blake, you're a good man—"

"Says who?"

"Oh, please. Cut the tough guy act. If you weren't a decent person, Mia wouldn't be here now."

"Neither would you," he said, a gleam stealing into his eyes.

He was right about that. If the child was in the state's custody, he'd have no need for nanny services. Life would be easier, but maybe her life wasn't meant to be easy. Maybe she was here for a reason.

"The thing is, I am here and you have to deal with me. Because I'm here, I have an obligation to that little girl asleep inside. You *are* a good man, or you'd have let the state of Nevada worry about her."

"I'm not so sure."

She decided to ignore that. His actions spoke louder than her words. "Now that you've taken her in, don't let it just be about a place to live. Go the extra mile and really help her. Make a difference in her life."

In her earnestness to convince him, Casey put a hand on his arm and felt the strength beneath the warm skin. The contact with him made her heart race again. "You'll feel good about yourself."

"Okay, sign me up." His voice was husky and deep and scraped along her nerve endings.

He reached for her and pulled her to him. It felt like slow motion but happened at the speed of light. She was in his arms and it was better than anything her imagination had dreamed up. He was all hard muscles and coiled strength before he lowered his mouth to hers. It was as if she'd been holding her breath for this since the moment she'd met him, and she couldn't stop the sigh of contentment. It was as if she'd waited all her life to feel Blake Decker's chiseled lips take hers, tasting like Southern Comfort and sin.

Her breasts were crushed to his chest as he held her against him with one hand, the fingers of his other hand snarled in her hair, angling her head to make the contact firmer, deeper, better.

He made a sound in his throat, part groan, part growl, but all male. She breathed in the spicy scent of his skin combined with the warm breeze off the desert, and the exotic mixture was like a drug coursing through her system. Discipline where he was concerned was a pipe dream. Soft sounds of approval drifted between them, and she was vaguely amazed that they were coming from her. But she couldn't seem to help it, because his mouth was doing delicious things to her mouth, her face, her ears, her neck. Good Lord, it was like a jolt of the best kind of electricity arcing through her.

They were both breathing hard, and she felt as if the heat was melting her from the inside out, fusing her body to his in the most wonderful way. She wanted to be even closer, needed to be nearer.

Just as she was praying it would never end, it ended. He seemed to freeze, then dropped his hands as if they suddenly burned.

"Casey…" He took a deep breath and ran a shaky hand through his hair. "That was my fault."

Fault? That meant that what quite possibly was the best kiss she'd ever had was wrong. Or he believed it was wrong, which was right. This *was* wrong because it was confusing and so very not right. If there was anything positive about what was happening, it was that none of those words came out of her mouth as she blinked up at him.

He moved back, far enough that he couldn't touch her. "That was inappropriate. You're my employee. I know better. I'm sorry."

He stared at her a moment longer, something dark and unreadable in his eyes. Abruptly he turned away and disappeared through one of the sliding glass doors to the penthouse master bedroom.

Casey touched trembling fingers to her lips, still moist from his kiss. He'd been right, of course, to stop. But, God help her, the distance he'd put between them didn't stop her from wanting him. And she couldn't decide which was more humiliating—that he'd put an end to it or that he was sorry he'd done it at all. It was fate or something that he'd finished what he'd started earlier.

Maybe it had been calculated to distract her. The plan had worked brilliantly, because she still didn't know why the Decker men had felt the need to protect Patricia from her daughter's child.

Even with suspicions running rampant, Casey was missing the warmth of just moments ago. It was still hot outside, but she was cold all the way through because she felt empty inside.

As wrong as it was, she still wanted him, just one more item in the long list of her sins.

Chapter Five

While Mia was in talking to the counselor, Casey sat in the waiting room—waiting for Blake. This was your standard issue area for hanging out. The chairs had a tweed seat on an oak frame and were arranged around the perimeter of the room. Walls painted in a serene shade of blue surrounded her, with generic seascapes hung here and there. A receptionist huddled behind a sliding glass window, probably looking at her watch every ten seconds to see if it was time to go home yet.

This was the last appointment of the day and Casey had called in reinforcements to set it up. Ginger Davis knew a lot of people in Las Vegas, and the counselor had worked them in two days after Mia's last disappearing act. Which also happened to be the same night Blake had kissed Casey on the terrace of his penthouse. *Kiss* and *penthouse* were two words she'd never expected to use in the same sentence regarding herself, but there it was.

Casey looked at her watch and noted that Blake was now officially a half hour late. She couldn't help wondering if his tardiness had anything to do with what had happened on said terrace, because she'd seen very little of him ever since. He was back to leaving early and coming home late. But he knew about this meeting with the counselor. Casey had called his secretary, who'd promised to remind him it was the last appointment of the day, making it easier for him to get here. And yet he wasn't here.

She'd tried calling his cell, but the call had gone to voice mail. Was he screening his calls? Because of that kiss? Or was it the fact that she'd drawn a line in the sand and made his presence here a condition of her continued employment? His not showing up would have to go under the heading of calling her bluff.

After exactly sixty minutes the door beside the reception window opened and Mia walked into the waiting room with Lillian Duff. The counselor was a small woman in her early to mid-fifties, with light brown hair and eyes. She wore square, black-framed glasses and looked as serene as the blue on her walls.

Casey stood and forced a smile. "So, how'd it go?"

"We got acquainted."

"Yeah, right." Mia rolled her eyes. "This is sooo lame."

"Feelings are good." Casey tried to put an optimistic expression on her face when she looked at the counselor. "It's best not to sugarcoat it, right? It's best to tell how you really feel."

Casey refused to pretend everything was fine. If that were the case, they wouldn't be here. If everything was hunky-dory, Blake would have made the effort to show up at the penthouse and take Mia to counseling, just the two of them, instead of standing his niece up.

"I have nothing to say." Mia flopped in a chair and folded her arms over her chest.

"Would you look at that open body language," Casey said.

"Bite me." The kid huffed out a breath.

"That's funny. When you ran away the other night and showed up at your grandparents, you had quite a bit to say. I'm thinking counseling is a good place to focus on what you'd really like to tell them."

"Dorks," she muttered.

Casey looked apologetically at Lillian. "She has issues."

"I noticed. Most kids who come to see me do." The counselor looked at her watch. "I see Mr. Decker wasn't able to join us."

"No." Multiple excuses flitted through Casey's mind, but she didn't say anything. It wasn't her job to monitor Blake or put a positive spin on his AWOL status. She glanced at Mia, who was putting a lot of energy into looking mad. "I'd like to make another appointment."

Lillian nodded. "For Mia and Mr. Decker?"

"Just Mia."

Casey set her anger on simmer. Blake was going to get his session, but it would be with her instead of the counselor. He was writing checks to both of them, so what the heck? Coming from her, it wouldn't be quite as politically correct.

Casey set up an appointment for the same time next week. Then she and Mia walked into the carpeted hall and headed for the elevator to the parking structure. She pushed the elevator button, and Mia turned away, slouching against the wall. The silence was deafening, worse than shrugs, eye rolling or name calling. It really fried her that all Blake had had to do was show up. He hadn't even had to say anything profound, because just being here would have said that he was invested in this child that no one wanted.

In all fairness, the Deckers were caught in a vicious cycle. Mia's inappropriate behavior was a cry for attention, but it made her hard to like and gave her uncle an excuse to push her away.

The elevator opened and Casey took a step forward so the doors wouldn't close. "Come on, Mia."

With the kid's back to her, all Casey could see was that she lifted a hand to her cheek.

"Hey, kiddo, we need to go."

Mia's thin shoulders hunched forward and she made a noise that sounded suspiciously like a sniffle. Casey held in a groan, but this was one more in a long list of reasons for her decision to specialize in the ten and under crowd. There was a world of difference between nine and Mia, who was going on thirteen. Hormones and feelings. Trauma and drama happened in that time and if a kid was at risk, this was when the behavior was most likely to show up.

Casey was used to dealing with kids pre-trauma and drama, when she could impact them in a positive way and head off the things that would send them down the wrong path. A path of destruction, like the one chosen by a kid she'd befriended in Baghdad. The seeds for his anger and frustration had been sown long before Casey met him, and dealing with Mia felt a lot like that.

But right here, right now, it was just the two of them and she had to do something. The question was what.

"Mia?" No answer. She waited, hoping the kid would blink first, but the standoff continued. "Are you crying?"

"No."

Casey moved away from the elevator and, when the doors closed, let it go. She walked over to the girl and stood there, but Mia didn't turn around.

"Hey, kiddo, talk to me."

There was no response, but the body language was dejected and unhappy.

Casey drew in a deep breath as she stuck her keys back in her purse and settled the strap more securely on her shoulder. She put her hands on Mia's thin shoulders and tried gently to turn her, but the kid resisted.

"I'm here for you."

"So?"

Casey was trying to pick up signals, but Mia didn't make it easy. It was hard to read between the lines when it was a single-syllable, one-word response, but Casey heard frustration, anger, hostility and, most of all, hurt. Maybe it would help if she could coax Mia to talk about it.

"Look, I think you know that your uncle is a busy lawyer. I'm sure something came up." Something like he absolutely had to make sure a married couple's relationship was severed between 5:00 and 6:00 p.m. today.

"Who cares about him?"

"Not me," Casey said, except maybe the part of her that felt guilty if the kiss she'd shared with him had in any way factored into his absentee status.

She should have stuck to her guns and not taken this job when her instantaneous attraction to him was off the charts. He'd kissed her, and she wished she could say she hadn't seen it coming. In hindsight she should have said her piece and walked away. In hindsight she wondered if deep down, she'd wanted him to kiss her. And now Mia was paying the price for her weakness.

"Look, Mia, I'll go out on a limb here and say that you obviously care about being stood up."

"You're wrong. I didn't want to talk to him, anyway."

"Okay. But wouldn't you have liked to *not* talk to him to his face?"

Casey turned the girl toward her, and the kid's eyes looked even more turquoise, because they were red rimmed. She had

to do something to comfort this child. It was always easy to
do that for the under-ten group. A hug. Kiss the boo-boo and
put on a Band-Aid and off they went. She was winging it with
Mia and felt as if she was skydiving and her chute hadn't
opened.

Still, she figured a hug couldn't hurt and tugged the girl
awkwardly into her arms. Mia stiffened and tried to jerk away,
but Casey hung on, refusing to let go. Somehow Mia was going to get the message that someone in this world gave enough
of a damn about her to acknowledge by comforting her that
this situation sucked a lot.

The battle of wills persisted for another thirty seconds,
which seemed like forever. Finally Mia relaxed into her and
buried her face in Casey's shoulder. The girl was only a couple
inches shorter, but a whole lot more lost, and the tug on
Casey's heart didn't go unnoticed. She was officially sliding
out of neutral and into the deep doo-doo of the affection zone.
This wasn't how it was supposed to go. *Darn it.*

"I'm here," Casey crooned, patting the shaking shoulders.
"It's okay. You're not alone, kiddo. And just so you know…"
She paused for dramatic emphasis, to make sure Mia was lis-
tening. "You're right. Your uncle is a dork."

There was a muffled giggle before the girl looked up.
"Told you so."

Casey pulled a tissue from her purse and handed it over.
"Are you ready to go now?"

"I guess." Misery still coated her from head to toe.

Casey couldn't remember wanting so badly to see a kid smile.
"How about on the way home I buy you anything you want?"

An unmistakable spark of interest appeared in Mia's eyes,
for just a moment chasing away the indifference she wore like
a favorite sweatshirt. "Anything?"

"Within reason." She put her arm around the girl's shoulders and led her back to the elevator. "Is there something you've always wanted?"

"A dog."

Holy Mother of God. But the more Casey thought about it, the more she liked the idea. A grin started slowly, then grew wider as Mia smiled, too.

"A man's best friend," Casey said as the elevator doors closed.

It was nearly nine when Blake rode the private elevator to his penthouse. He couldn't remember the last time he'd been this tired, but that was Casey's fault, which was his last thought before walking into his foyer where he found her standing. Kissing her had single-handedly sabotaged any restful sleep ever since, so it seemed somehow fitting that she looked ready to do battle.

And that was when he remembered that today was the counseling appointment he'd agreed to.

"Hi," he said, setting his briefcase on the floor. "How did the counseling go?"

Surprise flickered briefly in her eyes. "How do you know it took place? Maybe something came up and we forgot."

Along with the anger sparking in her eyes was a gleam of intelligence. Dealing with her would be much easier if she weren't so bright. But not nearly as entertaining.

"You don't forget anything," he said. "There's no doubt in my mind that you and Mia were there. And I wasn't."

"You're not even going to pretend it slipped your mind?"

He shook his head. "I was in mediation for a client whose financial settlement has been dragging on for close to a year. There was a breakthrough. Ending the session could have stalled things when we were on a roll."

"I see."

Her tone and the look on her face said that she didn't see

at all and that he was lower than the lowest life form. "Look, Casey, I know I—"

He heard something that sounded a lot like a throaty, deep bark just before a big yellow dog galumphed into the foyer. There was a clicking sound from its nails, which he knew couldn't be good for the expensive marble floor. Seconds later the animal peed on a leg of the table in the foyer, leaving a dark stain on the rug underneath. Just then Mia came racing in and skidded to a stop when she saw Blake, uncertainty in her big eyes.

He glanced from her to Casey as shock, surprise and anger rolled through him—in that order. "If I lived in the suburbs, I could see where it might be possible for Old Yeller to end up in my house. But this is the top floor and without opposable thumbs, I'm pretty sure it couldn't use the key card in the elevator."

"She's not an 'it.' Blake, meet Francesca. Frankie," Casey said to the dog, "meet Blake, your new dad."

"You brought this beast into my home?"

"It's Mia's home, too." Determined, Casey lifted her chin slightly. "She followed the rules and went to counseling, even though it was lame, dorky and sooo stupid. She was there in good faith, so I thought a reward was in order. She's always wanted a dog. Did you know that?"

"No."

"Well, it's true. So I agreed."

"I don't and I'm reversing that decision."

"No, Uncle Blake. Please let me keep her." Mia went down on one knee and put her arms around the dog, which nuzzled her cheek. "I promise she won't be any trouble."

"Too late." He looked at the dark spot on the rug. "She has to go. I mean leave."

"You can't do that," Mia cried.

"I already did," he said.

"Mia," Casey moved to the two of them and scratched the dog's head. "It would be best if you let me talk to your uncle. Show Frankie her bed in the laundry room."

"But—"

"Now," Casey said. "Make her comfortable, secure and accepted in her new environment."

Blake was pretty sure there was a message in those words for him, but he refused to feel guilty. He lived here, too, and last time he checked, the money for all this came out of his bank account.

He walked through the foyer, into the family room and straight to the kitchen, where he grabbed a beer from the refrigerator. After twisting off the cap, he took a long drink and let the cold, bubbly bite slide down his throat to his empty stomach. *Damn the torpedoes and let the chips fall where they may.* Fireworks were imminent, because Casey was right behind him.

"There's no way I'm telling that child she has to give up the dog."

He looked down at her. "You don't have to. I already did."

"Reversing *that* decision is the least you can do to make up for being such an ass."

He set his beer on the kitchen island and stared at her. "Excuse me, but I could have sworn you called me an ass."

"If that's your way of giving me a diplomatic out for what I said, forget it. I stand by the words and will say them again. You're an ass. The dog stays. And, if I have to, I'll take you on."

"You'll take me on?" His eyes narrowed on her, and damned if the thought didn't flash through his mind that she was beautiful when she was angry. "I'm a lot bigger. No way you can take me."

"Don't forget, I've had hand-to-hand combat training. I

know three hundred ways to incapacitate or kill an opponent with my pinkie."

"Right." His mouth twitched, but he refused to give in to the amusement. He was being ambushed in his own home. First Mia and now a dog? "The thing is, I've got the law on my side since I'm the boss."

"There's the law and then there's human decency." She put her hands on her hips and stared at him, anger rolling off her in waves while her chest rose and fell. "I'm fully aware that you sign my paycheck. I agreed to take this job, but you were present and accounted for when I made it clear, more than once, I might add, that you're the one on probation. If you're not willing to put the time in for your niece, give me one good reason why I should."

"Listen, Casey—"

"No," she said, pointing at him. "You listen. Oh, wait. You weren't there to see or listen when she tried to hide the fact that she was crying because you couldn't be bothered to show up."

He didn't like the guilt her words dredged up and went on the offensive. "So you let her bring Lassie here? That fixes everything."

"At least the dog will stick by her. It's more than she can count on from you."

"When Francesca can pay room and board, we'll talk."

"What about establishing a relationship with your niece? Your sister's child?"

Stirring up the past was throwing salt in the wound and he really didn't like that. "I have a job to do. Clients are counting on me."

"Taking cover behind the profession won't hide the fact that you're anti-relationship. A lone wolf doing his best to keep from bonding. You're so anti that even your career choice is all about ripping relationships to pieces."

"You've never been married. Otherwise you'd realize that I don't bring marriages down. But when they fail, each party has the obligation and prerogative to have their rights protected."

"Maybe. But there are a lot of demanding professions that don't get in the way of family responsibilities. You put in an awful lot of hours—or it could be that's just an excuse to dodge the hard work at home." She shook her head, and anger turned to pity on her face. "No wonder your marriage didn't work out."

"My marriage didn't work out because my wife cheated on me with my best friend." The memory of that still had the power to enrage him and it was fueled further by the fact that it did.

She looked momentarily startled. "I'm sorry."

The same two words he'd said to her the other night, after crossing the invisible line and kissing her. He'd decided the best course of action was to forget it had ever happened. *Yeah, right.* But maybe they should talk about it and clear the air.

"Look, I'm sensing a little hostility, and if it has anything to do with what happened the other night—"

"What happened?" She blinked. "Is that the correct legal term for a kiss?"

Okay, so maybe bringing it up wasn't the brightest idea he'd ever had. "Look, I've already apologized for that. I was hoping we could move ahead and forget about it."

"Is this some kind of strategy they taught you in law school? When you're sinking like the *Titanic,* create a distraction, and maybe no one will notice you just plowed into an iceberg?"

For a hotshot attorney who used words like Old West gunslingers used six-guns, this conversation, which he'd initiated, was going badly. His only defense was that he couldn't get that kiss off his mind. The taste and texture of her lips were pretty spectacular and made him want to do it again. And again. Frankly, memories of that kiss made him want to do far more than kiss, which was a formula for disaster.

"Casey, I promise you it will never happen again."

"You promise?" Her face had *skeptical* written all over it. "Is that like the promise you made to give me time off for my class?" She tapped her lip as her eyebrows pulled together in mock thoughtfulness. "Or maybe this is like the promise you made to go to counseling with Mia."

He had no defense. If she was a jury of his peers, he was guilty as charged. "I give up."

"There's a surprise."

"What does that mean?" he asked.

"It means you haven't even tried. It means relationships take work, and so far I haven't seen you work at anything but lip service. It means that if you're not willing to make an effort, Mia would be better off in the system."

"That's fairly heartless. If that's how you truly feel—"

"What? You'll fire me?" She pressed her lips together and stared at him as if coming to a decision. "I will not stick around and watch the hurt in that little girl's eyes over and over again when the only person she has in the whole world can't put her first even once. You can't fire me, Blake. What you can do is find yourself another nanny—because I quit."

Chapter Six

When Casey turned and left the kitchen, she was shaking, but it wasn't all about being angry. All the while she was busting Blake about broken promises because he'd vowed not to kiss her again, her female parts were hoping he'd forget about that decision not to kiss her again. And didn't that just make her the world's biggest hypocrite? It was also a very good reason to go far, fast.

"Casey, wait—"

She wanted to ignore the request. For God's sake, she'd quit thirty seconds ago. Her insides were doing an energetic high five. All except her heart. The problem was that when she let her heart rule, bad stuff happened. She kept walking.

"Casey, please, I need to talk to you."

Damn. Damn. Double damn.

She stopped and turned to face him in the hall just outside

her room. Behind the closed door next to it, she could hear Mia talking to Frankie.

She met Blake's gaze. "We got her from the animal shelter."

"Who?"

"Frankie. If no one claimed her, she was going to be put down. It was Mia's idea to rescue a dog no one wanted, instead of getting a designer pet. Her words."

"I see."

"She's crying out, sure. But she's a good kid with a good heart. If you spent any time with her, you'd know that. But as long as I'm the nanny and you sign my paycheck, the odds are slim to none that that will happen. So I'm leaving."

"Without two weeks' notice?"

"Yes. So sue me. You're a lawyer." She turned away, fully intending to walk into her room.

"And if I promise to get to know her?" The look she shot him when she glanced over her shoulder must have contained sufficient sarcasm, because he added, "I know my track record doesn't inspire trust. And you're right about me taking advantage of your being here to shirk my responsibility to my niece. But I can change."

She turned and folded her arms over her chest. "Why should I believe that?"

"Because I got a reminder of what it's like to be in this on my own, and it scared the crap out of me."

What got her attention was the fact that he'd admitted to being scared. It was a clear violation of some macho code known only to men, where it was a major show of weakness to actually declare out loud to a woman that you were anything but in complete control.

She narrowed her gaze. "You're lying."

"Why would you say that?" Indignation shone in his blue

eyes, turning them to an intense shade that was almost navy. He settled his hands on lean hips, which made her notice how perfectly his wrinkled white dress shirt fit his flat abdomen and broad chest. The long sleeves were rolled up to reveal wide wrists and strong arms dusted with dark hair. It wasn't the breach in the macho rules she noticed now, but her all-too-female response to his masculinity.

"Why would you accuse me of lying?"

Because she wanted an ironclad reason, one without perceptible wiggle room, to stick to her guns and quit. "It's what lawyers do. Only you call it strategy. Or spin. Or reasonable doubt."

He nodded, but the dark look didn't budge. "I can't force you to believe me, but I can ask for another chance to show you I'm sincere. I'd like you to stay."

It was on the tip of her tongue to say no, but the hum of Mia's voice made her remember the kid's valiant attempt to hide how hurt she'd been at being abandoned at counseling—before she dissolved into tears. The good news was she could still cry, which was more than Casey could say for herself. The other good news was that the behavior was a sign—a sign that it wasn't too late to do some good. And that had been Casey's vow, to help her make sense of the mess she'd made in Iraq. She'd promised to dedicate her life to helping kids find the right path.

She needed to put up or shut up.

"Okay. I'll stay if the dog can stay." She pointed at him. "And you're still on big-time probation."

"I'll agree to be on probation if the dog is, too," he agreed.

"You're such a lawyer."

"Negotiation is one of my best skills." He let out a long breath. "And in the spirit of new beginnings, I'm sorry I missed the counseling session. I'll tell Mia the same thing."

"Good." She shot him a sympathetic look. "And you think I've been hard on you. Brace yourself."

"Okay. So we have a deal?"

"We do. Let's give this one more try." She sighed. "And if you can be magnanimous, how can I do less? I'm sorry I called you an ass."

"Apology accepted."

He grinned, and her heart was high-fiving, while her gut twisted with disapproval that she'd caved. There was little question in her mind who the ass was now.

A few days after she did a one-eighty on her decision to leave, life in the penthouse settled into a routine of summer school and doggy chaos without another major meltdown. Blake had been on his best behavior: he'd made it home for dinner each evening and he'd attended the rescheduled counseling session, which Mia had pronounced "lame." It was the new norm, and so far Casey was happy she'd decided to stay.

She was puttering around the kitchen while Mia surfed the Net, learning about canine care, when the phone rang.

"Hello," she said after picking it up.

"It's Pete with building security. There's a lady here who says she's Mr. Decker's mother, Patricia. Shall I send her up?"

Shock was Casey's best and only explanation for giving the okay. So much had happened since the night Mia had run away that Casey hadn't given much thought to Blake's parents. She was trying to figure out how to tell Mia that her grandmother was here when the bell rang and Frankie raced to the door and started barking.

"Who's there?" Mia asked, kneeling down on one knee to hold her dog.

"Your grandmother." Before the girl could comment, Casey opened the door. "Mrs. Decker, won't you come in?"

"Thank you, Casey."

"It's nice to see you again." Casey closed the door and let out a long breath. "This is a surprise."

They say clothes make the man, and if there truly were equality of the sexes, that would apply to women, as well. Patricia Decker was wearing a copper-colored shell, slacks and a matching jacket in a style that Casey recognized immediately. It was a brand touted as being able to hold up during travel. You could practically double knot the material, throw the garment in a suitcase and fly around the world, and it would look like it had just been pulled from the closet. The woman wearing it was another story.

Blake's mother looked ill at ease. And the dark circles beneath eyes the same turquoise color as Mia's clearly indicated that she'd been to hell and back. Still, every brunette strand of her shiny bob was perfectly in place. Diamond studs, which were almost certainly the real thing, twinkled in her ears.

Casey held out her hand. "Let's go sit in the living room."

"Do we have to?"

So much for a cooling-off period. Mia's antagonism seemed to roll off her in waves. A few minutes ago she'd been carefree and happy, trying to do the right thing by her dog. The change back to angry and hostile was startling.

Casey tried to be über-polite to compensate. "Mrs. Decker, why don't we—"

"Call me Patricia, please."

"All right." Casey held out her hand to indicate they should sit down. "Can I get you a cold drink?"

"Don't be nice to her," Mia protested. "She didn't give a crap about whether or not my mom and I were thirsty. Or cold. Or hungry."

Patricia's lips compressed into a straight line before she took in a shuddering breath. She looked at her granddaughter and said in a voice just above a whisper, "You look just like your mother."

"Is that supposed to make me like you?" the girl said.

"I didn't know you were here—"

"Before or after you threw my mother out and then she died?"

"Mia, that's enough," Casey admonished.

The girl glared at them. "Why should I believe she didn't know I was with Uncle Blake?"

"For what it's worth, Mia, I don't agree with what your grandfather did."

"He's not my grandfather."

"Technically speaking, he is." The older woman sighed. "He's your mother's father."

"Not after he threw her out. And I don't believe you didn't know about me," the girl said. She was hugging her dog as if the animal were her lifeline.

Casey sympathized with Mia, but that was no excuse for bad behavior. "Mia, you're being rude and that's not acceptable. The fact that your grandmother is here says a lot."

"She's here because she wants something."

"Whatever her reasons, I expect you to treat her with courtesy and respect," Casey shot back. "If you can't do that, a time-out is in your immediate future."

"You're sending me to my room?" the girl said doubtfully. "Like a little kid?"

"That's the way you're behaving," Casey agreed. "It's the way you'll be treated until you learn good manners."

"Lincoln was right. You do have spunk," Patricia said.

"I picked it up when I was a little girl with older brothers." And why the heck would she share that with Blake's mother? She must be more nervous than she'd realized. The woman wasn't here to see her. "Mia, I'd like you to apologize to your grandmother."

"It's all right." Patricia had been staring down at the girl, but the words got her attention. "The fact is, she's right. I do want something."

"I knew it," Mia said smugly.

Casey shot her a look. "What can we do for you?"

"I'd like to invite you to dinner," Patricia replied.

The statement was directed to Casey and she didn't know what to say. So she used the technique she'd learned from Blake. Distraction. "Do you think enough time has passed to qualify for a cooling-off period? It's not really a mediation if all the parties involved aren't present."

"It's not about arbitration. Mia has every right to be displeased. Just so you know, we didn't throw your mother out. We disapproved of her boyfriend and she ran away."

"My father?"

"Yes."

"He's a dork, too."

Patricia nodded. "I was heartbroken at losing my child and went into a deep depression. Then we learned she'd passed away and you'd gone to live with distant relatives. I struggled again, coming to terms with the fact that I'd never be able to make things right with my daughter. It took me a long time to come around. Your grandfather was trying to spare me from another episode."

"Doesn't make it right," Mia said.

"No, it doesn't. He was wrong to keep you from me, but I understand why he did."

"Whatever."

"Obviously, talk is cheap and won't change the past," Patricia said. "All I'm asking is that the three of you come to dinner."

Casey was pretty sure that meant her, not the dog. "That's very kind of you."

"It's not kind."

"No kidding," Mia interjected.

Instead of being aggravated, Patricia smiled. "Again she's right. My motivation is selfish. Whether you believe me or not, I simply would like to get to know you. Will you come?"

"I'll let Blake know about the invitation and have him call you," Casey answered.

"Fair enough." Patricia looked from Casey to her granddaughter. "Thank you for seeing me and I'll say goodbye."

Moments later she was gone, but definitely not forgotten.

"Old bat," Mia mumbled before going to her room, with Frankie trotting eagerly after her.

Casey's head was spinning. Didn't that just figure? Today no one had run away from home or neglected to show up for an agreed-upon counseling session. Her boss hadn't kissed her or in any way indicated that he thought of her as anything but the hired help. It had been a trauma-free day in the child-care business, but heaven forbid that there should be any peace.

Blake had given his secretary strict orders to schedule his day so that he could be home in time for dinner at 6:30. Today was a close call, but he hadn't missed an evening meal with Mia since Casey had almost quit.

He wasn't ready to slap a "success" sticker on the arrangement yet, but he was even less prepared not to find Casey in the penthouse with his niece. The thought of her waiting for him sent a vibration through his system that was part awareness, part anticipation. And all heat.

Mia's nanny was an incredibly interesting woman. Alternately tough and tender. Glib and gorgeous. It was saying a lot that he appreciated her way with words more than the awesome way she filled out a pair of jeans. When she was around, he found himself watching the graceful movement of her body and waiting to see what she'd say next. On top of that, by some miracle, she seemed to be able to keep his niece under control. He'd be a fool to give Casey any reason to quit again, including, but not limited to, kissing her. Again.

In the lobby of his building, he slid his key card into the private elevator slot and rode the elevator to the penthouse, suddenly eager to be home. And when he walked in the door, Mia, Casey and the dog were all waiting. They started talking, and barking, all at once, and he was able to hear only the words *mother, dinner, witch, poison* and *no way*. The last words were followed by a bark from Frankie.

Blake held up his hands. "Time-out."

"I won't do it," Mia said. "You can't make me."

"Take a time-out?" he asked. "If you don't, I won't even hear what I can't make you do."

"She's an old witch who's trying to buy my goodwill. I'm not falling for her act."

"Careful, Mia," Casey cautioned. "She's your uncle's mother."

"So we're talking about your grandmother," he said to his niece.

The girl folded her arms over her chest and glared defiantly at him. "No way."

"Way." Blake shrugged. "Biologically she is your mother's mother, which makes her your grandmother."

Mia started to argue the irrefutable, and the thought crossed Blake's mind that she might make a good attorney someday. But not today. When Casey jumped into the fray, he held up his hands again.

"One at a time, you two. I have no idea what's going on." He pointed to Casey. "You first. Sorry, kid, but age has its privileges," he added when the girl opened her mouth to protest.

"Mia's grandmother stopped by today." Casey shot the

girl a "zip it" look when she made disapproving noises. "She came with olive branch in hand."

"I'd rather eat an olive branch raw than have dinner at the dork's house."

Blake set his briefcase by the door and Frankie trotted over to sniff it. Warily Blake grabbed the handle and set the briefcase on the foyer table. The dog gave him a "drop dead, bastard" look that reminded him of his niece. Then he focused back on the conversation. He was guessing "the dork's house" was his parents' place.

"Start at the beginning," he advised. Being a divorce lawyer and listening to two people with opposite points of view were good training for everyday power struggles. He looked at Casey. "Again, you go first."

"Figures," Mia mumbled.

To her credit, Casey refused to engage and ignored the comment. "As I said, your mother stopped by today. Without calling."

He was curious why she added that. Was it a problem for her? But that would only delay the exchange of information, so he said, "Go on."

"She invited us to dinner. Including me," Casey added. "I'm not sure why."

"My dad thinks you're spunky." Blake figured he and his dad had something in common. They both liked Casey.

"I won't go." Mia glared at him. "If she thinks I can be bought for the price of a rice grain and a dry crust of bread, she's wrong."

"Very dramatic. I don't suppose it would do any good to point out that there are children in the world who would consider that a feast."

Mia huffed out a breath and rolled her eyes.

"I didn't think so," he said. "Maybe the dorks want to get to know you."

"If the old guy did," Mia answered, "he wouldn't have pretended I don't exist."

"He didn't do that. Children's services contacted him about you first and he turned the matter over to me."

"He gave them a big no and said nothing to my...to her."

"We didn't think it through," Blake admitted.

"I get it," Mia said. "He didn't want Lady Dork to get her panties in a twist. And that will make me want to see them why?"

"You're family," Casey said. "This could be the beginning of a meaningful bond."

"Right." Mia's voice dripped sarcasm. "They're probably in trouble with the charity police and look bad for ignoring a grandkid."

Blake folded his arms over his chest. "Maybe they haven't handled this whole thing in the best way, but they're reaching out now."

"So?"

"So," Casey joined in. "I think it's safe to say that you've blown through your share of relatives because, frankly, you're not all that easy to get along with. Can you really afford not to at least accept their dinner invitation?"

"They're your mother's parents," Blake said.

The girl looked at them, standing side by side and presenting a united front. "Yeah, I get it," she finally said. "That makes them Grandma and Grandpa. Biologically. But they don't act like it."

Blake watched Mia and a feeling of déjà vu swept over him. He remembered his younger sister, the rebellious girl who had questioned everything. She'd been difficult, but also smart, funny, beautiful. He'd loved her and now she was gone. The only part of her left was this child, who was resisting a relationship with the people who, in her opinion, wronged both her mother and her.

Part of him couldn't blame her. The folks had handled this badly. He didn't know what had happened with them and his sister, but current and past history convinced him that what transpired had most likely been handled with the finesse and sensitivity of a herd of water buffalo. But Casey was right. The kid didn't make it easy to like her.

"Look, Mia," he said seriously, "my guess is that your grandparents want to get to know their only grandchild. Maybe they miss their daughter." He wouldn't be surprised. He missed his sister.

"I'm not going to take her place," the girl argued.

"No one expects that," Casey told her. "They're just reaching out."

"So what? It's too little, too late."

When Frankie bumped her nose on Casey's leg, Casey absently rubbed the dog's head. A minute later she stopped and Frankie nudged her hand, indicating she wasn't yet finished being rubbed.

"It's too late for your mother," Casey pointed out, her tone sympathetic. "But not for you. You don't want to look back and wish you'd given them a chance when there was time. They'd probably like to go back and change how they acted and what happened with your mom. None of us get through life without regrets about things we've done."

Blake was watching Casey and noticed the shadows that slid into her hazel eyes, turning the gold flecks to brown. It didn't take a PhD in psychology or expert credentials in body language to see that she had regrets in a very big way. He wondered what could possibly have happened to make her look like that, so sad and guilty. Casey was talking to Mia with the voice of experience, but the kid's next words showed that she wasn't getting the message.

"I don't like them."

"You don't even *know* them," Casey pointed out. "Get acquainted, and then you're allowed to have an opinion on whether or not they're worthy of your respect and affection."

"They won't like me." Mia's unhappy expression spoke volumes.

Casey got it, too. "I see we're getting to the real reason behind your behavior. Fear of rejection."

"I'm not afraid—"

Casey held up her hand. "It was just an observation. I don't blame you. But you have to take some responsibility for your behavior. I said before, and I'm not being mean, you don't make it easy to care about you. If you're rude and mouthy, it gives people a reason to brush you off that isn't about rejecting you as a person."

Blake had some experience with rejection as a person. His wife had turned to another guy, and not just anyone. His closest friend had ended up in her bed. He'd done his best to give her what she wanted and it hadn't been enough.

"There's a lot of truth to what Casey is saying." Blake knew the kid didn't like hearing that. "And you've got plenty of reasons to feel the way you do."

"Then I don't have to go—"

"I didn't say that." He held up his hand. "I want to talk to Casey about this before I make up my mind."

"Mia, why don't you take Frankie out for a walk?" Casey met his gaze. "You probably aren't aware of this, but there's a dog run in the complex. And Pete with building security will keep an eye on them."

"Okay." Blake looked at his niece. "You heard Casey."

The kid wanted to object, but apparently the safety-in-numbers rule applied, because she looked at the two adults, who stood shoulder to shoulder, then wordlessly got the dog's leash and left with the animal.

Blake ran his fingers through his hair. "What do you think?"

"You get to make the decision. I'm the hired help. You're the man of the house."

The fact that he was a man was never far from his mind when he looked at her. Right now he couldn't take his eyes off her mouth, and his hands itched to discover every part of her. He wanted to explore the lips he had only touched for seconds yet couldn't manage to forget. The depth of her appeal was uncharted and the effort to keep from charting it was taking a toll on his willpower.

"Still," he managed to say, "I'd like your opinion. Will dinner with my folks help or hurt Mia?"

Casey shook her head. "I don't have my crystal ball on me at the moment. The fact is, not even an expert in child psychology could answer that question. Best guess?"

He'd take her best guess over expert opinion any day. "Absolutely."

"I think Mia is protesting too much. She's the one who started this scenario in motion by showing up at her grandparents. Her actions are saying, 'Notice me.' But her defiance is about protecting her feelings. If they don't like her, she can say she was right. She told us so."

"Then we should call her bluff and meet the folks halfway?"

She nodded. "If for no other reason than it covers your backside."

"Excuse me?"

"I'd give your mother a call and accept the invitation so that in the future Mia can't blame you for keeping her from her family."

Casey ran her tongue over her lips and he couldn't see

anything except himself kissing her. Suddenly it seemed like the blood from his brain headed to points south of his belt and all coherent thought stalled.

"Point taken," he managed to say. "And I agree."

When Casey smiled, he was far too happy that she'd approved of his answer. And when he managed to use his brain for rational reflection again, he would try and figure out why that was so important.

Chapter Seven

Dinner at the Deckers' could be more awkward and uncomfortable, but Casey wasn't sure how. Blake was doing his best to keep the conversation going, but Mia was sullen and uncooperative and wouldn't engage, even though the older couple had fixed a kid favorite, burgers and fries. Lincoln and Patricia would probably need a triple dose of cholesterol-lowering meds after serving fat-heavy foods to thaw their granddaughter's cold feelings.

Clearly that had been Patricia's intent when she'd come by the penthouse to issue the invitation. Even Lincoln was on his best behavior, conciliatory and subdued compared to the last time Casey had been here. His wife had probably given him a talking-to and he'd gotten the message.

The five of them were sitting around a dining room table long enough to land a jumbo jet, and the dark wood looked sturdy enough to hold the weight. A matching breakfront and buffet took up a lot of space in the big room. Delicate china, silver and crystal looked beautiful and dignified on a light green linen tablecloth. The formal setting seemed at odds with the menu, but it convinced Casey that the older couple was trying. So far the kid wasn't cutting them any slack.

"That was one of the best burgers I've had in a long time." Casey glanced from one end of the table to the other, at their host and hostess. "Do you barbecue often, Lincoln?"

"We have a housekeeper who does all the cooking," Patricia answered. "I gave her the night off so it would just be family."

Her husband set his cloth napkin on the table. "I forgot how much I enjoy it."

After yet another uncomfortable silence Blake cleared his throat. "I don't grill anymore, either. And I used to be pretty good at it."

"You've been able to get home for dinner more often lately," Casey said, meeting his gaze across the expanse of table. "You should try it again."

"Maybe I will." Blake glanced at his niece, to Casey's left. "What do you think, Mia? Steak or chicken?"

"Whatever." She slouched lower in her chair.

Casey noted with amusement that she'd eaten a good-size burger and an impressive number of fries for a kid who couldn't be bought with a grain of rice and a dry bread crust. Maybe the fact that she'd enjoyed the food served by the very people she'd vowed to hate was partly the reason for more attitude than usual.

"Let Mia and me help you clean up," Casey offered.

"That's very kind of you." There was a strain in the smile Patricia settled on everyone around the table. "Dessert, anyone? I have the makings for ice cream sundaes."

Casey knew that was one of Mia's favorites and looked to

her left for a reaction. Eagerness gleamed in the girl's eyes for a moment; then it disappeared, replaced by a deliberate mask of bored indifference.

"Mia?" Patricia looked at her granddaughter. "Do you like ice cream?"

"Not much."

"Oh." Disappointment clouded the older woman's expression. "I thought it would go best with a casual dinner. Probably I should have asked what you preferred."

Casey was starting to feel sorry for the Deckers. They had made a lot of mistakes, no question about that. But the fact that this couple, who were probably more the pheasant-underglass type, had served burgers and fries seemed like an obvious sign that they wanted to make amends. It didn't appear that Mia planned to bend anytime soon, so maybe a little help in that direction would be in order.

"Patricia, do you have pictures of Mia's mom?" Casey could feel the glare from the girl and the startled look from Blake. She ignored both.

"Yes." The older woman looked grateful, then glanced at Mia. "Would you like to see them?"

Before the kid could snap out an abrasive response, Casey said, "That's a great idea."

"I'll go get them." Patricia pushed her chair back and stood.

"Let me help," Lincoln offered.

Casey caught Blake's eye and said, "Why don't you give your folks a hand? Mia and I will clear the table."

Blake looked doubtful but said, "Okay."

When they'd carried a load of dishes to the kitchen, Mia said, "This is so lame."

"Including the food?" Casey set the plates in the sink, with Mia's empty one on top. "Let's go get the rest."

Mia did as asked, but if she'd moved any slower, she'd have gone backward. When they had the table cleaned off and the dishes arranged in the dishwasher, Casey leaned back against the cupboard.

"Do you want to talk about it?"

Mia glared. "I can't believe you made me come here."

"Technically, it was your uncle who made the decision." Casey remembered the expression on Blake's face when she'd said he was the man of the house. Even now the hungry look in his eyes made her shiver. But that wasn't something to deal with now. "He thought it was important for you to know your family."

"This is so wrong." Mia slumped against the island, elbows on the top, and rested her chin in her hands.

"I know you're angry and you have every right to be," Casey said. "But they can give you something no one else can."

"What? Nothing?"

"No. Memories of your mom." Sadness and regret rolled through her. "Take it from me that's something you're going to want."

"What do you know about it?" The misery in her expression took away the hostility in her words.

"When I was just about your age, my mother died of cancer. Just like your mom."

Mia's eyes filled with pain. "Do you still miss her?"

"Very much. And photos are all I have of her." This child didn't need to know that Casey's father had withdrawn and hadn't even shared himself after her mom died. "Your grandparents are reaching out. You don't have to let them off the hook. It's okay to make them accountable, but don't cut off your nose to spite your face."

Mia's mouth curved up just a fraction. "What does that even mean?"

Casey laughed. "Old expression. It just means that refusing to look at pictures of your mother will just punish *you* in the long run."

Mia stared at her for so long that Casey thought she'd refuse. Finally she nodded. When they turned, Blake was standing in the doorway with a bemused expression on his face.

"You did this to me," Mia said as she walked past him.

Casey looked at him and shrugged. "No good deed goes unpunished."

"Tell me about it." He rubbed the back of his neck as he stared after his niece. "I heard what you said."

"I figured."

"Have you ever heard the saying that people come into our lives for a season and a reason? Or something like that."

"Yeah."

"I can't help feeling that way about you."

"Oh?" Her heart started to pound. *Darn it.*

"Yeah. I'm fairly sure there are other nannies with strong child-care credentials and an impressive skill set. But your background gives you an empathy someone else might not have."

"Yeah."

She remembered thinking something similar at their first meeting, when her heart had gone out to the motherless girl. What she hadn't realized then was how the rest of her female parts would respond to her boss. It didn't make the assignment impossible, but it certainly challenged her in ways she'd never been challenged before. And the way he was looking at her now didn't help.

"You're a remarkable woman, Casey." He folded his arms over his chest. "You're good with Mia and not afraid of my parents. That's quite a combination."

The intense expression in his eyes wasn't exactly employer-employee relationship-friendly. It was more approachable, and then some, tearing down any obstacles that stood between. She didn't claim to be an expert in the field, but even she could see it was similar to the way he'd looked before kissing her.

And how he could kiss. But since then she'd found out his wife had cheated on him with his best friend. She'd been warned.

She knew why he didn't do personal relationships, why he wouldn't commit. That was important for her to know in case she was tempted to kiss him again. Like now. They were just beginning to make headway with Mia. Why jeopardize it by pursuing something doomed to go nowhere?

He stuck his fingertips in the pockets of his worn jeans. "I just want you to know that I've noticed."

Right back at you, she thought. But probably what she had noticed wasn't what he meant. "Speaking of your parents and Mia, we should probably go see what's going on."

"You mean be Switzerland?"

She smiled. "Just in case."

In the sitting room there was a big stack of albums on the coffee table. Patricia was sitting on a love seat in front of the fireplace, with Mia beside her and Lincoln resting on an arm.

"Here's one of your mother at just about your age," Patricia was saying.

The girl pointed to the picture. "Is that Uncle Blake by the pool?"

"Yes." The older woman laughed. "This was snapped just before April pushed him in."

Mia glanced up and grinned at Blake. "You were beaten by a girl."

He walked over and sat on the other arm of the love seat, the one closest to Mia, so he could see the photo. "I remember that. She caught me by surprise."

"Yeah. Right," Mia said.

"She was such a mischievous child," Patricia said wistfully. She glanced at the girl beside her. "You look a lot like her, Mia."

"You said that before."

"And now you can look at the pictures and decide for yourself." Patricia turned the page. "Here's another one of April and I swear it could be you. There's a very strong resemblance."

"I guess." Mia turned the page. "How old was she when this one was taken?"

Casey watched the Deckers pore over the family photos and felt good. Really good. Maybe Blake was right about her coming into their lives at just the right time. She'd wanted to turn down the job, not break her personal rule about kids of a certain age. But this was a good day with a positive outcome. She'd convinced Mia to meet them halfway for this moment in time. Would another nanny have been able to connect? She would never know.

Just like she would never know what connecting with Blake would be like. He wouldn't go there. And if he did, she'd be a fool to go there with him.

Blake opened one of the sliding glass doors connecting his bedroom to the terrace and stepped outside. It was a beautiful August night and the breeze that skipped over the lighted pool water picked up a little coolness. It was after midnight and he had a busy schedule the next day. Nowadays he had to cram the same work into fewer hours in order to make it home for dinner. He should get some sleep. If he could, he would, but thoughts of Casey wouldn't leave him alone long enough to rest.

There was a movement from one of the sliding glass doors on the other side of the terrace, near the room where she slept. And suddenly there she was. *Casey. Speak of the devil…* Although the way the moonlight turned her blond hair silver made her look more like an angel.

She was wearing pink cotton pajama bottoms and a thin-strapped, very un-angel-like white knit top that clung to her small breasts like a lover's hands. The image was sexy as hell—and not one he'd ever expected to have of a nanny.

But that was before he'd hired Casey.

She moved farther onto the terrace and stopped by one of the green wrought-iron patio tables, resting a hand on one of the matching chairs. Staring out at the lights of the suburbs intersecting with the glitz of hotel-casinos, she let out a deep, sad sigh. He wasn't sure what made him characterize it as sad, except that her shoulders slumped and she was frowning. He'd grown accustomed to her smile, spirit and sass, and missed them now. This introspective side of her made him even more curious.

If Blake was as smart as everyone thought, he'd go back inside before she realized she wasn't alone. When he took a step out of the shadows and into the bright moonlight, some part of him knew his brain wasn't the organ responsible for the decision.

"Casey?"

She gasped and pressed a hand to her chest as her gaze swung in his direction. "Blake. Good grief, you startled me."

"Sorry."

She stared at him for several moments, catching her breath. "I didn't mean to wake you."

He shook his head. "You didn't. I just couldn't sleep. What's your excuse?"

"Same."

"Insomnia epidemic." He stood beside her, the sleeve of his T-shirt brushing her bare skin. "I was thinking about my folks. And Mia." That was partly true. "I really appreciate what you did tonight."

"It was nothing."

"On the contrary. Like the song says, you were a bridge over troubled water."

"That's why you're still awake. Can't get the tune out of your head," she teased.

"Nope. Not the reason." When their gazes connected and held for a moment, a spark of sexual awareness passed between them and her eyes widened slightly, telling him she'd felt it, too.

She leaned away, as far as she could without taking a step. *Never show weakness.* "I'm glad you're happy with my work, Blake, but don't make more out of it than I deserve."

"You orchestrated a photo marathon with my family and I'd say that deserves quite a bit of praise. Although, for the record, I could have done without the photographic history of my geek stage, and I plan to initiate a covert op at my earliest convenience to search out and destroy all evidence of it."

She didn't laugh, which was a surprise. Normally she got his sense of humor. "In my opinion you never had a geek stage, like the rest of the human race."

"Right." He was glad she didn't think so, which meant her opinion mattered more than it should. "The thing is that somehow you convinced Mia to look at those albums with her sworn enemies. It was a miracle."

"Not a miracle. I'm no saint," she argued, self-incrimination lacing her voice. "Far from it."

The vehemence in her protest was sincere and forceful and out of proportion to the woman he'd come to know, which meant there was something about this woman he didn't know. "Why so hard on yourself?"

"I don't think I am. Just keeping it real. About myself and the job. To do it to the best of my ability, I need to achieve a level of emotional distance."

He could use some of that emotional distance right now,

because the sight of her toned arms and smooth skin was tying him in knots. She was a striking woman. She was pretending that the commitment and drive she focused on Mia were just part of the job. But he didn't buy it. She cared deeply, and that made her even more beautiful to him. The length of her neck, the curve of her cheek, her turned-up, freckle-splashed nose all tempted him to do what he'd promised not to do. More than taking his next breath, he wanted to kiss her—and somehow he had to distract himself.

What had she just said? *Oh, right.*

"Uh-huh," he said. "You were very objective and unemotional when you got my niece a dog. You could have fooled me."

"Not being fooled is the goal." There was a far-off expression on her face, as if she were halfway around the world. "Observation. Evaluation. Objectivity. Don't get sucked in. I learned the lesson well in the army…" Her voice broke and she turned away.

"Casey?" Blake put his hands on the bare flesh of her arms and felt her trembling. "What is it?"

"Nothing." But she was still shaking.

It wasn't like her to bring up that time in the military. Was it his teasing remark about a covert op? He'd been exaggerating, but she'd gotten specific.

"What happened in the army?" he asked.

She bent her head, and though he couldn't see her face, the movement was fraught with emotion and defeat.

"Nothing."

"I can tell by the way you're trembling that it's not nothing. Talk to me."

"There's nothing to talk about. I'm fine. Just tired. I'll be able to sleep now…" She tried to pull away, but he wouldn't let her go.

He turned her and the single tear coursing down her cheek shone silver in the moonlight. "You're crying."

"No, really—"

"Don't." He cupped her face in his hands and brushed his thumb over her cheek. "I know tears when I see them."

Misery was stark in her eyes. The longing to take away her pain joined with the need to taste her, and suddenly he couldn't fight it anymore. Blake lowered his mouth to hers. The light touch was hot enough, but what really sent nuclear blast-type heat billowing through him was Casey's soft sounds of pleasure and surrender.

A heartbeat later his ability to draw in air went from zero to not enough oxygen in the universe, and Casey was breathless, too. He thought about stopping, was working up to it when she put her hands on his chest, but the feel of her touching him decimated his willpower and took rational thought with it.

He curved his palms on her hips and drew her close as he kissed her lips, cheeks, jaw and neck. He nibbled a spot just beneath her ear as he brushed the tiny straps of her shirt out of the way and down her arms. The top pooled at her waist and—*thank you, God!*—she wasn't wearing a bra. His fingers ached to touch her and in a nanosecond the soft flesh of her breasts was in his hands.

He bent his head and drew her left nipple into his mouth and heard her sharp intake of breath as he sucked her deeper. Her breathy little moans heated his blood and sent it pounding through him, roaring in his ears. As he kissed her, they turned toward the moonlight, mining all the romance from the night. He wanted to see her in the glow of Mother Nature's glory and lifted his head.

And that was when he saw the red puckered scars that marred her midriff and disappeared beneath the waistband of her cotton pants. The sight was more horrifying because it was completely unexpected. He knew she felt his shock, because she tensed and a heartbeat later pulled out of his arms and turned away. Quickly she slid her arms through the straps and righted her shirt to cover herself.

"What happened to you?" he whispered, his voice hoarse and harsh. "Don't tell me nothing."

"I don't want to talk about it."

"Maybe you should," he said.

She turned back and shook her head. "I made a bad call. Like now."

He ran his fingers through his hair and blew out a long breath. "A slip in judgment. A broken promise."

"Yeah." She met his gaze and there was hurt in her eyes. "Not completely your fault. I'm a big girl. I can take care of myself. Been doing it for a long time."

"I didn't plan for it to happen."

"Don't worry. I know it wasn't like that. I'd never accuse you of anything."

"That's not what I'm worried about. It's just…" He didn't know how to say what was on his mind. "I don't want to take advantage of you."

"I remember. You're anti-relationship and a woman shouldn't expect a commitment."

"You make it sound like a tagline." He settled his hands on his hips. "Just so we're clear, I didn't pick a career based on ripping relationships apart. I was happily married, or so I thought. I was good at negotiating settlements—assets, money, alimony, visitation agreements, kids, even dogs. Not once did anyone ever talk about the love. It's all animosity and lots of it. The thing is, if the bitterness is that big, the love must have been, too, but no one tells you where it went. My wife struck the first blow when she slept with my best friend, but the love took a long time to die."

"Look, Blake, I'm not asking why. You don't owe me an explanation. You have a past and so do I. This isn't a good idea for so many reasons. The most important one being Mia."

"Oh?" His head was so messed up, he wasn't exactly sure what his niece had to do with anything.

"She's making strides. Maybe that's too ambitious. Baby steps. But I see progress and it's not a good idea to do anything to upset that. We need to channel all our energy into her."

"Right. Okay." He nodded a little too willingly.

She cocked her thumb over her shoulder in the direction of her bedroom. "I'm going in now. Good night."

Moments ago he had been in heaven, but now it pretty much was hell. And he blamed himself, the lust he'd let get out of control, what with his lack of a personal life. He'd been telling himself that would get better when everything with his niece stabilized.

He wanted to believe that what just happened was no big deal, but he'd also wanted to believe that his wife hadn't cheated on him. He'd especially wanted to believe that his best friend hadn't been involved. He'd been wrong then and he was afraid he was wrong now. But that didn't put the brakes on his lust. Or his curiosity.

The scars were evidence that something had happened to Casey, and he couldn't shake the feeling that the damage inside her was far worse than what he could see. But she'd refused to give up her past.

If there was one thing a divorce attorney saw over and over, it was that secrets had a way of not staying secret.

Chapter Eight

The day after kissing Blake, Casey continued to be appalled at how easily he'd gotten past her defenses. She had faced danger every day in Iraq and had the scars to prove it, but the fact that he could make her forget everything, including those scars while he exposed them, really scared her.

"I miss Frankie."

Casey glanced over at Mia in the passenger seat of her car. After she had picked Mia up from summer school, the two of them had gone to lunch, then stopped at an office supply store for Mia's project paraphernalia. The class would be over soon and the final assignment was a good portion of the grade. So they'd decided to dazzle the teacher with materials and color. Browsing every aisle of the warehouse-size store had been time-consuming. It was nip and tuck whether or not they would beat Blake home for dinner.

"I'm sure Frankie misses you, too," Casey assured her.

"Yeah." Mia looked worried. "But when she's alone too long, she gets into trouble."

"Not unlike someone else I know," Casey teased.

The girl rolled her eyes. "I never got in the trash and dragged it all over the place."

"True." Casey signaled a left turn into the luxury condominium complex. "And I don't believe you've ever grabbed grapes from the bowl on the kitchen counter and eaten them off the floor."

"But she had consequences," Mia pointed out. "Her tummy was upset, because dogs aren't supposed to eat that stuff."

"Who do you think really suffered?" Casey glanced over. "Frankie did not keep that gas to herself."

"No, it was pretty stinky." Mia giggled, a happy and age-appropriate sound not heard as often as it should be.

God bless that dog, Casey thought.

After pulling into the complex and parking, Casey noted that Blake's car wasn't there yet. Then Mia grabbed the white plastic bags with school supplies from the backseat and they rode the elevator up to the top floor. Even before Casey fit her key into the front door, the dog was barking a welcome on the other side of it.

"She knows we're home," Mia said happily.

Casey wasn't so sure. Could be the dog thought they were breaking in. But when the door opened, Frankie was right there, looking up at Mia with adoring brown eyes. The girl dropped to one knee and gave her pet a hug.

"Hi, Frankie. Did you miss me? Were you a good girl while we were gone?"

Casey gave them a moment and walked through the foyer and into the family room. It was hard not to gasp at the sight of Blake's open laptop computer lying haphazardly on the carpet, with the keyboard letters scattered around. She looked closer and the damage indicated that the dog had repeatedly pawed the fragile electronic device until the keys came off. After her initial thought that this wouldn't go over well with Blake, her next was that he didn't usually leave the thing out. He normally used it in his study.

Her third realization came when she heard the front door open and close. It was unfortunate that they'd spent so long picking out Post-it colors, because there might have been time to hide the evidence and break the bad news to him more gently than the visual he was going to get.

"Hi, Mia," she heard him say. The dog must have jumped on him, because his next words were, "Frankie, get down."

Casey quickly scooped up the plastic keys and tried to push the wounded computer under the coffee table. She heard footsteps on the marble floor behind her and sighed.

"What the hell happened?" Blake's question confirmed that her efforts were too little too late.

She looked up from where she was kneeling in the ruins of what had once been a state-of-the-art portable computer. Now it was little more than a dog toy. Before she could answer the question, the doggy perp ran into the room and pawed at what remained of the keyboard.

Mia followed and flopped on the floor, throwing her arms around the dog. "It's not her fault."

"That's what all the doggy delinquents say." Blake looked furious. "That excuse is followed closely by accusations of abuse and neglect."

"Maybe it can be fixed," Casey said, her heart sinking when she looked at the keys in her hand—Tab, Caps Lock, Shift and Control.

"Fixed?" Blake asked incredulously. "There's a better chance of negotiating a lasting peace in the Middle East." His voice was deadly calm, too dead and too calm. He looked at Mia. "Why is it out here?"

"I saw it here this morning. You must have been working last night and left it here," Mia said.

Casey watched the muscle in his tight jaw jerk and wondered what was going through his mind. Memories of kissing him last night had been looping through hers all day. But he was a guy and probably hadn't given it another thought.

"It belongs in the study," he said, neither confirming nor denying. "How did she get the thing open?"

"She's smart?" Mia said, part statement, part question.

Casey stood and met Blake's gaze. "Obviously it was left open."

"No." All statement, no question.

It left no room for debate, but Casey didn't take the hint. "We've had this conversation before. Unless Frankie grew opposable thumbs, her canine abilities are severely limited. There's no way the dog opened the laptop."

"You left it open," Mia accused him.

"I don't do that," Blake responded just as stubbornly, and the glares between uncle and niece were almost identical.

"I bet when you were growing up and did bad stuff, you always blamed it on my mom."

"I have no independent recollection of that," he said.

"Look at it this way," Casey suggested. "When you're in court and you need an excuse for the judge, you can tell him the dog ate your computer."

"Not funny."

"I thought it was," Mia said, unsmiling, as she stared at him. "You're going to make Frankie leave."

"It's crossing my mind as we speak," he confirmed.

"You can't do that," she cried.

Casey agreed with her but had a feeling their reasons were very different.

"She's a good watchdog," Mia said.

"Who's going to watch *her?*" he shot back.

Mia thought for a moment. "She helps the housekeeper."

"What?"

Mia's chin lifted defiantly. "Crumbs on the floor. She cleans them up. Better than the vacuum."

"It's true," Casey agreed.

"The nanny isn't supposed to take sides," he reminded her.

"I'm not doing that," Casey lied. "Just being a witness to the truth. Frankie waits for someone to drop food and it barely touches the floor before it's gone. Environmentally she's a benefit."

"Right," he said, his voice dripping sarcasm. "No taking sides there."

"She's good to talk to," Mia continued. "She always listens and doesn't argue or talk back."

He folded his arms over his chest. "So she's a good role model for you?"

"Yes," Mia said. Then it sank in. "I don't argue or talk back. Anymore," she added.

"Except now," he pointed out.

Mia's eyes were suspiciously bright as she rubbed a finger underneath her nose. "She just wants to love you."

"You mean she wants to love *you.*" Blake shook his head and blew out a long breath. The anger seemed to drain out of him. "This can't happen again."

The girl's expression turned eager. "It won't. I swear, Uncle Blake."

"Why should I believe you?"

"If she does anything wrong, you can ground me for the rest of my life."

Casey saw his mouth twitch and noted the way he brushed his hand over the lower half of his face to hide the fact that he wanted to smile.

"Please don't make her go away," Mia begged.

"Okay, but here's the deal," he said. "She's your responsibility. That means if you want to keep her, you have to walk her, feed her, care for her and not let her destroy stuff."

"I promise." Mia stood and slid her fingers under the dog's collar to lead her down the hall. "You won't be sorry."

"Wait. There's more," he said.

She stopped and looked warily at him. "What?"

"You need to attend your grandparents' anniversary party in a couple of weeks."

"This is blackmail," Mia protested.

"I know." He grinned. "And you've done a really good job of making a case for the dog to stay. You might want to consider a career in law."

"If I consider it, will you let Frankie stay and not make me go to the party?"

"Not a chance, kid." He was enjoying this. "This is the deal. Not only will you voluntarily go to the party, but you will be gracious to your grandparents and everyone there. You'll say please and thank you. No slouching, shrugging or rolling your eyes when you disagree with anything."

"But, Uncle Blake—"

He held up a finger to stop the words. "No arguing. No negotiating. Those are my terms. Yes or no?"

She released a big sigh, rolled her eyes, shook her head and finally glared, but eventually said, "Deal."

"Okay, then. Frankie can stay."

Without a single gesture or word that could jeopardize her pet, and before he could change his mind, Mia left the room with her dog and the door down the hall slammed behind them.

Blake grinned at Casey. "I think I'm getting the hang of this whole parenting thing. Who knew it was so easy to control the kid?"

"She's right about the blackmail thing," Casey pointed out. "Would you really make her get rid of the dog?"

He rubbed a hand over his neck. "I considered it, but did you see the tears in her eyes?"

"Yeah." But she hadn't realized he'd noticed.

Casey realized the man actually had a heart and it was really soft. And she was in a whole lot of trouble. If the sexy five o'clock shadow on his jaw hadn't convinced her, the fact that he wouldn't have followed through on his threat to get rid of the dog would have.

He might be getting a handle on parenting, but Casey was losing the battle to resist him.

Mia stomped into the penthouse foyer after coming home from their counseling appointment and glared at her uncle. "You only think about yourself."

Blake stared angrily back at her. "I don't claim to be an expert in raising kids, but one thing I'm learning, if something I do sends you into brat mode, it must be right."

"I hate you," she said, then turned and went down the hall, the dog on her heels. The next sound was the door to her bedroom slamming.

"Okay." Casey set her purse on the entryway table, wishing for the silence on the ride home, which had been the calm before the storm. "Feel the love."

Blake leveled his scowl on her. "I thought you said counseling would help. Her attitude is worse than ever. For crying out loud, all I said was no to a stop at the mall. Why does that put me at the top of America's Most Wanted?"

Casey folded her arms over her chest and tried to ignore

the fact that in his worn jeans and T-shirt he looked really hot. Not heat hot because it was August and this was the desert, after all. Hot as in she wanted to feel his lean, muscular strength and his manly flesh pressed against her. Preferably while they were both naked. The image did nothing to help her focus on negotiating a peace.

"She's not angry about the mall. It's about painful feelings that were stirred up. You probably already know this, Blake, but counseling doesn't work like aspirin for a headache. It's more like surgery. Open up your guts and take out the bad stuff, with all the pain of recovery and no meds to take the edge off it."

"Gee," he said. "Remind me again why I listened to you and agreed to go?"

"Because I threatened to quit."

"Right."

Still using the medical analogy, she realized there was a reason doctors weren't encouraged to treat family members. It was called losing objectivity due to personal involvement. As if she hadn't known she'd done just that after the first kiss, Casey really got the message when she didn't stop him from getting her naked from the waist up. She should have quit way before Blake agreed to counseling in order to get her to stay.

He blew out a long breath. "Would you like to take a walk?"

Bad idea. Really bad. "I should start dinner. And I should be here if Mia needs to talk."

"I need to talk to you." He met her gaze. "I can make it an order."

"Not necessary. You're the boss." Why couldn't she have remembered that when they were drenched in moonlight and his mouth was on hers?

When she returned from telling Mia where they were going, he opened the front door and held out a hand, indicating that she should precede him. After a ride in the penthouse elevator, they went through the building's luxurious lobby and turned right into a hallway, then walked past the his and hers spas and out the door next to the workout room.

The grounds at One Queensridge Place were as impressive as the rest of the complex. An Olympic-size pool was surrounded by chaise longues and patio tables, but there were also cabanas, tentlike areas for a little extra seclusion. Casey glanced up at Blake and the intensity in his profile instantly bumped up her heart rate. Seclusion with him would be dangerous in every way she could imagine.

After they passed the tennis courts, they reached a walking path that was bordered on either side by palo verde trees and vibrant desert plants blooming in red, yellow, pink and purple. It was after six in the evening and the temperature was still in the nineties, but the air was pleasant, as opposed to July's oppressive heat.

At intervals along the winding path, ornate wrought-iron benches had been placed for anyone who wanted to sit and chat. When Blake indicated she should take a seat, she did. Casey didn't want to, but an order was an order. Unfortunately he did, too, and when his leg brushed hers, a quiver started between her thighs that not even an order could stop.

"So, what do you want to talk about?" She folded her hands and rested them in her lap.

"I don't understand why she's so hostile," Blake began. "In the session things started out okay, then went downhill when the counselor brought up her mother."

"Did you talk to her about what happened when her mom left home?"

"I can't."

"Sure you can. I know it's difficult and painful, but you can give her the facts."

"No. I mean, I really can't, because I don't know the facts. I was away at law school when April got pregnant. I didn't witness the events." He leaned back and extended his arm across the back of the bench.

Casey slid as far away from him as she could get and struggled to keep a clear head, what with his nearness scrambling her brain. "So, you're saying that during that time you never spoke with your folks? You didn't call home? Come back for Christmas? Or summer?"

"Of course I talked to them."

"Your sister's name never came up? Patricia and Lincoln didn't dump on you about the crap that was going on with their daughter? Your sister?"

"Yeah, they said she'd taken off. But I was never clear on whether or not she was thrown out or just took off with her boyfriend when she got pregnant."

His mother had implied that Mia's mom had rebelled when she'd been forbidden to see the guy her parents didn't like. "And you didn't bother to find out what actually happened?"

The look he turned on her was filled with dark intensity. "I was up to my ass in law review and classes. My sister never contacted me and I thought she was making a life for herself."

If Casey had been in the same predicament, her brothers would have found her. There was no question in her mind about that. They would never be accused of sensitivity overload, but they'd have made sure she was okay. The Deckers made her family look like communication central.

Casey weighed her options. She could be honest and say that or sugarcoat it and keep from getting fired. What made up her mind wasn't a desire to retain her job, because just a while ago the thought had crossed her mind that leaving would have been best. Telling him anything less than what she truly thought was a waste of breath. She owed it to him and Mia to call it like she saw it.

"I think the truth is that it was easier for you to believe your sister was okay than to get involved."

His fingers curled into his palm. "You have no idea what I believed."

"Not specifically. But I know how you are now, what your priorities are. Work comes first. In my book, family members should look out for each other. You can't phone it in like you did with your wife."

"Wait a damn minute. What does that have to do with anything?"

"It's your pattern and it didn't happen overnight. College, law school and career are all excuses for turning your back on the personal, painful, messy stuff. The stuff you don't want to do."

"That's ridiculous. I wanted to stay married. My wife knew I was focused on building a law practice—"

"You say focused. I say workaholic."

"Whatever. She knew how I was when we got married. Later she changed the rules. She thought she could make me a different man, and when she couldn't, she found another one."

Casey folded her arms over her chest and met his gaze. "Why does that surprise you?"

"What?" He blinked.

"You spent more time with your secretary than you did with your wife, the woman you loved. She wanted to see more of you."

"If she'd told me—"

"Oh, please, Blake. Look at the way you are now. When you hired me, you promised to be here the nights I had a class, and the very first time you broke your word. That behavior started a long time ago."

"Who died and made you the psychology queen?" Anger glittered in his eyes.

"My mother, actually. And I'm no professional. I can only tell you how I felt about it. My dad didn't know what to do with a little girl who cried every night for her mother, so he ignored me. When kids are ignored, they'll do whatever they can for attention and approval. I'm sure you realized that I was the only one of his kids to follow in his footsteps and join the army."

"Yeah, I got that," Blake said.

"Mia wants your attention."

"She hates my guts."

Casey shook her head. "She hates that her mother got cancer and died. She hates that she and her mom were abandoned. Caring and being dumped again would be pretty high up on her list of things not to do. So it's easier to lash out and push you away. It's easier to make you not like her. But hate you?" She shook her head. "I don't think so."

"From here in the cheap seats, I'd say you're wrong about that."

She'd certainly been wrong before. *So wrong,* she thought, remembering the innocent face of the Iraqi teenager she'd befriended. Once before it had been her belief that a sincere desire to help could erase all the bad stuff, but her naiveté had been the means to an unspeakably evil end and innocent people had paid the ultimate price.

And here she was again, going above and beyond the call of duty. For what? Her job was child care, but where did she draw the line? Physical well-being? Or did she try to make a difference by building a bridge from Blake and Mia's past to their future? Was this a hill she wanted to die on?

"Like I said, I can only tell you what happened to me. Rather than deal with me and my grief over losing my mom, Dad hid in his cave. Maybe he handled his own grief that way.

I have no idea, because he never talked to me about it. I'm saying that Mia really just wants an explanation. Your instinct is to fix things and you can't in this case. So you're hiding."

"Whoa. I showed up for counseling—"

She held up her hand. "I'm not saying you didn't. But there are lots of ways to hide from things you don't want to deal with. Work is one. My point is that I can't make you come out. But with Mia under your roof and doing negative things to get your attention, there's no way you can pretend that she's okay."

"Don't hold back, Casey. Tell me how you really feel." He stood up.

"Look, Blake—"

"I think I'm talked out." The look in his eyes was somewhere between angry and confused.

Then he turned and walked away from her without another word. Casey watched until he and his excellent butt disappeared around a curve in the path. Her heart ached for him and his niece.

And for herself.

Apparently what had happened to her overseas hadn't been enough of a lesson to keep her from getting in over her head. The next time she went for a walk with Blake… *Halt. About face.*

There wouldn't be a next time. Heart-to-heart talks were not in her job description. And from now on she needed to remember that this was just a job.

Message received, but following the order would be tougher to pull off.

Chapter Nine

Casey returned to the penthouse after a Sunday visit with her dad and felt as if she were going back and forth between caves. The highlights of dinner conversation with Nathan Thomas had been politics, sports and a rousing debate on whether or not this was the hottest summer on record for Las Vegas.

For her it had been, but that had nothing to do with how many days the thermometer had registered one hundred degrees or more. From the moment she'd met Blake Decker, awareness and heat had ruled her world. And today she'd wished her mother were still alive to talk about things. She'd thought about confiding in her dad. She'd even mentioned Blake and Mia, and he'd said that she looked happy, that working for the guy must agree with her. Reading between the lines, Casey had realized he only wanted the fairy-tale version of her life, not the problems. Yet another way for him to hide.

She let herself into the penthouse, set her purse, sunglasses and keys down, and listened. The underlying hum of the air conditioner was all she heard. No voices. Not even the TV.

That was weird.

The television was Blake's primary defense system in his cave. Whenever he was alone with Mia, he had a gazillion channels of programming between him and an actual conversation with his niece. Casey had suggested he come out of hiding and have an honest-to-goodness conversation about the kid's mother, but there was no historical behavioral evidence to indicate that he would actually do it.

Casey walked down the hall to Mia's room, which was her hiding place. Surprisingly the door was open. That never happened, except when the girl wasn't in there. Like now.

Clothes were scattered on the plush beige carpet and across the pink-and-green floral comforter, along with the iPod that was usually attached to the girl's person. Papers and books littered the white desk. It all looked normal, except that Mia wasn't sprawled across the bed, looking hostile and bored.

There was no indication here of whether or not Casey should be worried, so she reversed direction and headed to Blake's home office, her next stop. But in the family room she caught a glimpse of movement outside and walked to the sliding glass door. In a navy blue tank suit, Mia pushed herself up out of the pool to retrieve a blow-up beach ball. And she had a big grin on her face. Blake was in the shallow end, his broad, bare chest visible above the choppy pool water. He was smiling, too.

This had all the makings of an alternate universe.

Casey opened the sliding door and walked outside. The sun was descending on the other side of the building, leaving the terrace in shade. "Hi."

Mia's smile widened with genuine pleasure. "Casey! I'm glad you're back."

Definitely an alternate reality in which there was no hostility. "I'm glad to be back. What have you two been up to?"

Blake moved from the middle to the side of the pool and looked up at her. "Come on in. The water's fine."

"I'm not wearing a bathing suit."

"Go put one on," he suggested.

"Haven't got one," she lied and the look on his face told her he knew. Exposing her scars wasn't high on her list of things that constituted a good time. There would be questions that she didn't want to answer.

Mia moved beside her. "Uncle Blake took me to Red Rock Canyon. We did the scenic drive and stopped at the visitor center. Then we went to LBS, the hamburger place at the Red Rock Casino, Resort and Spa. The burger was as big as my head."

"Really?"

"An exaggeration," Blake said. "She has a pretty big head."

"Look who's talking," Mia retorted, then threw the ball and hit him squarely in the chest.

A good shot, Casey thought, *but what a fabulous target.* The contour of tantalizing muscles was sprinkled with a dusting of hair, which tapered to a place hidden beneath the waistband of his swim trunks. Her palms tingled and the sensation was all about an intense yearning to brush her hands all over him. The oh-so-tempting thought made her back up a step.

She turned her attention to the girl, who'd jumped back in the pool. "So what did you think of Red Rock Canyon?"

"It was so awesome." Mia tipped her head back and wet her long hair to get it out of her face. "The red in the rocks is really pretty."

Casey squatted down by the edge of the pool. "You don't suppose that's how it got its name, do you?"

"No." Mia rolled her eyes in a nonhostile, oh-brother kind of way that was so incredibly normal.

Casey felt a little bubble of satisfaction expand inside her. Blake had taken an interest in Mia and it showed in the girl's softening attitude. He'd taken her advice and come out of his cave. It had made a difference, at least for today, and that made her happy and proud.

"Did you see anything at the visitor center about it being named by a man?" Casey asked, feigning innocence.

"You mean because of the red color running through the rock formations?" Blake asked, eyes narrowing.

"Yeah."

"Are you implying that men have no imagination?"

"Pretty much," Casey admitted. "And I don't mean that in a bad way. It's straightforward. You know exactly what it is. Or where you are. For instance, a street that runs into a home improvement store could be called Home Improvement Boulevard."

His grin made her stomach pitch and roll as surely as if she were on a ship during the storm of the century. Ribbons of desire floated and curled through her, making it a challenge to draw air into her lungs.

"And women are so much better at calling a spade a spade?" he asked.

"Of course. Have you ever noticed how clever the names of hair salons are?"

"Such as?"

"A Cut Above." She tapped a finger against her lip as she tried to think of more. "And A Wild Hair."

"I've got one," Mia said, floating on the ball. "Hair Raisers. And Hot Headz Hair."

"Right. Good for you," Casey said, praising her.

"Figures she'd remember names like that," Blake complained good-naturedly.

"What about Curl Up and Dye?" Casey suggested.

He folded his arms over his chest. "Oh, that's cheerful."

"D-y-e," she spelled out. "Hair Today Gone Tomorrow."

"Creative," he agreed, "But counterproductive."

"Hair Four U," Mia chimed in.

"Hey, two against one," he protested

"So speaks wimp boy," Casey taunted.

"Them's fightin' words."

"I used to be a warrior," Casey reminded him. "Is that a challenge?"

A gleam stole into his eyes. "I'm just saying…"

Casey started to stand and back away, but she wasn't fast enough. Blake grabbed her almost before she saw him move. Strong fingers gripped her hands and tugged her forward, into his arms. Surprise pushed a shriek out of her; with her mouth open, she swallowed water. She came up sputtering and pressed against the world-class chest she'd practically drooled over a few minutes ago.

Laughing, Blake steadied her. "For the record, brute strength trumps cleverness."

"No fair, Uncle Blake."

Mia sneak-attacked him from behind. She grabbed his shoulders and tried to push him under but couldn't manage it. Because he was caught by surprise and thrown off balance, Casey added her weight to the assault, and the girls were able to take him down.

When he surfaced, Casey said, "*That's* two against one."

Retaliation burned in his eyes as he hooked his hands beneath Mia's arms and tossed her into deeper water while she shrieked with delight.

Then Blake turned on Casey. "Cheaters never prosper."

Casey laughed as she eased backward, toward the steps and escape. "That wasn't cheating. It's known in the military as overwhelming force."

"I'll show you overwhelming."

He dove into the water and wrapped his steely arms around her legs as he positioned her midriff on his shoulder. Seconds later he had his feet beneath him and was standing with her hanging over his back. The sudden move surprised her, but this alternate view of his butt wasn't bad at all. Casey wanted to squeal with delight, but her motivation was far different from Mia's.

"Okay, Hercules, you made your point. You can put me down now." The tone seriously lacked conviction.

"Throw her in like you did me, Uncle Blake." Mia was grinning.

"Hey," Casey cried. "Whose side are you on?"

Blake half turned and gave the girl a thumbs-up. "She knows which side her bread is buttered on."

"So it's true what they say." Casey tried to wiggle free but he was too strong.

"What do they say?"

"Blood is thicker than water," she answered.

"Yeah." He shifted her off his shoulder and into his arms.

The early evening breeze in the desert was pleasantly warm, unless you were wearing wet clothes. Casey shivered and he felt it because he was still holding her.

"You're cold."

Without waiting for an answer, he walked to the shallow end shelf and stepped out of the pool and onto the concrete deck, carrying Casey as if she weighed nothing. If that wasn't enough to make her feminine heart go fiddle-dee-dee, nothing would. And then in true hero mode he grabbed one of the big, fluffy towels on the table and dragged it around her shoulders.

"Thanks," she said through chattering teeth.

Mia joined them and he wrapped her in the remaining

towel. Obviously Casey was using his and she didn't miss the thoughtful gesture.

The girl freed her long hair from its terry-cloth confinement. Her thick, dark lashes were wet and spiky and made her turquoise eyes look even bigger and more beautiful. But the coolest thing was the fun shining in them. "You know, Uncle Blake, I've been thinking—"

"That's a dangerous prospect," he teased.

Mia grinned without an eye roll. Imagine that. "Seriously. I've been thinking about the anniversary party—"

He pointed at her and faked a stern expression. "You're not getting out of going, so you can stop thinking."

"A little advice," Casey offered, her shivering under control. "Don't spread that message to the youth of America."

"Will you guys listen?" Mia demanded. "If I have to go, I think Casey should go, too."

"A rousing endorsement." Casey tucked wet hair behind her ear. "It's not in my job description and I'm not part of the family."

"Boring." Mia's mouth puffed into a pout. "At least if you come, it will be a little fun."

"Woo hoo," Casey said. "Way to change my mind."

"You should go," Blake agreed. "My dad likes you."

"Because I'm perky. Or was it plucky?"

"I think he said spunky, but that's beside the point." Blake folded his arms over his chest. "The folks would love to see you."

"C'mon, Casey," Mia pleaded. "Say yes. Don't make me go alone."

Casey sighed. "This is piling on. And I have to say the whole 'blood is thicker than water' thing is darned annoying."

"That means you'll go. Right?" Mia asked.

"That means I'll think about it."

Although she hadn't said a solid yes, Blake and Mia gave each other a high five as easily and naturally as if they'd been doing it for years. That was the good part. The bad? She'd practically agreed to go to a family function that was over and above her regular duties. She tried to tell herself that it was all part of the job, but she wasn't buying that.

She was getting pulled in emotionally as easily as Blake had tugged her into the pool. Her life felt like quicksand, and every step she took, every maneuver, every day with the Deckers made her sink a little more deeply.

If she didn't extract herself from this situation, there would likely be hell to pay.

Three days later, after her summer school finals, Casey stopped by the home office of the Nanny Network president. She'd called earlier to make sure it would be okay and now waited after ringing the bell. Moments later the door opened.

Ginger Davis smiled. "Come in, Casey. It's nice to see you."

"Thanks for letting me come by."

"It's important." She shut the door and led the way through the beige travertine-tiled foyer and into the living room.

The spacious area, with a white sofa and a glass-topped coffee table, was serene with soft lighting. Floor-to-ceiling windows overlooked the lights of the valley but screened out the bustle of Las Vegas far below. The room was luxurious and suited her boss, an elegant woman with an address in one of the city's most recognizable buildings.

Ginger's red-highlighted brown hair was pulled away from her face and restrained with a rhinestone clip. Even dressed casually in crisp denim jeans and a white cashmere sweater with three-quarter-length sleeves, she would have a hard time passing for ordinary. But that didn't mean her life had been easy. Rumors about her past circulated, and the compassion in her eyes hinted at a history full of speed bumps. Right now she exuded welcome and warmth, which made what Casey had come to say that much easier to relate. Then she remembered what Ginger had said moments ago.

"How do you know it's important?" Casey asked, sitting on the edge of the overstuffed sofa cushion.

"Because this isn't normal business hours and you didn't want to discuss it over the phone."

"Right." She folded her hands and settled them in her lap. "Big clues."

Ginger slid back into the plush cushions and tucked her bare feet up under her. "You're stalling, Casey. Just tell me what's bothering you."

So many things, not the least of which was facing the fact that she was a coward. This side trip to see Ginger was what the army classified as running for cover.

Casey took a deep breath. "I can't work for Blake Decker any longer."

"I see."

The words were spoken in a soft, calm voice but did nothing to soothe Casey's concerns, especially when Ginger didn't say more. The silence stretched between them, a management technique to gather information, because a nervous employee felt compelled to fill the silence. Casey didn't bite, mostly because she didn't want to share further information unless absolutely necessary. So they stared at each other until the other woman blinked.

"Is there a reason you want to leave?"

Casey nodded. "It's not working out."

"I'd appreciate it if you could be more specific."

That would mean admitting that she was making the same mistakes after promising herself it wouldn't happen again. She'd vowed to remain objective, but kissing Blake had made detachment impossible. So she only said, "I agreed to take this job on a temporary basis. As a favor to you."

"I'd hoped time with Blake Decker would change your mind." Ginger sat up straight, her eyes widening. "Did he do something to make you uncomfortable?"

"No." That wasn't exactly true, but not the way the other woman meant. And part of the reason Casey wanted out was because of how badly she'd wanted him to kiss her and how much she wanted more. It was wrong and she wasn't sure how to keep from going there if she stayed.

"Did he come on to you?" Ginger asked. She frowned and slid forward on the sofa. "He did. I can see by the look on your face. There are laws against that sort of thing. He's an attorney and should know better than that. The Nanny Network has an attorney on retainer. I'll contact him, and Blake Decker will wish he'd kept his hands to himself—"

"No," Casey said. "It wasn't like that."

"How was it?"

It suddenly became absolutely necessary to share further information.

Casey had hoped to make this quick and easy, but now knew that wouldn't work. Ginger saw too much, and she, Casey, would have to come clean.

"He did nothing inappropriate."

"But he did do something?"

"He kissed me. Twice," Casey replied.

"And if you're taking it out of the inappropriate column, that means you were okay with it."

"Yes." Casey waited two beats, then said, "And no."

Ginger sighed. "What's going on, Casey? Talk to me. I can't help if you don't give me the facts."

"The fact is that I'm attracted to him," she admitted miserably.

Very attracted, she added to herself. So much so that he filled her thoughts during the day and her dreams at night.

And she'd never been a starry-eyed, dreamy sort of woman. This was different, something she couldn't seem to control.

"Okay," Ginger said.

"See, that's the thing. It's not okay. It crosses a line. It's a problem."

The other woman looked thoughtful. "Is it impacting your ability to care for Mia?"

"No. In fact she asked me to go along when the two of them attend an anniversary party for Blake's parents. She's not, shall we say, enthusiastic about going and said it will be more fun with me there."

"Sounds like you're bonding with her."

Casey nodded. "That probably happened when I helped her pick out Frankie—"

"Excuse me?"

"The dog. Francesca. We call her Frankie." Casey had to smile at the memory of the ill-fated laptop. "Anyway, Mia was pretty upset when Blake blew off counseling, and she wanted a dog."

"I see."

"He's improving, though," she added quickly. "They attend sessions once a week, and he's home for dinner every night now. He also makes it a point to be there for his niece when I have a class or my weekend afternoon off."

Casey remembered coming back to the two of them having a great time in the pool and pulling her in. Literally. In the beginning she could have walked away unscathed. Now she had feelings for the little girl and the man. If history repeated itself, somehow it was going to blow up in her face, and she was here to prevent that.

"So," she continued, "you can see that it would be best for me to quit working for him."

Ginger looked a little shell-shocked. "What I see is that the

Deckers are making progress in family bonding. Thanks to you, as far as I can tell."

"They're doing better." But Casey refused to make it about her.

"I don't have to tell you that every child needs stability to thrive."

"No, you don't."

The last child she'd befriended had only known violence, and Casey had believed kindness and caring could undo that state of mind. She'd been so wrong and others had paid the ultimate price for her mistake. It was imperative that she get out before anyone got hurt.

"I also don't have to remind you that because of her past Mia Decker needs constancy more than the average kid."

Casey sighed. She so didn't want to hear that. Not long ago Mia had said that her uncle would dump her like everyone else. And there was a very real possibility that leaving Blake's employ would fall into that category for the kid. This whole mess could be filed under the heading "damned if she did, damned if she didn't."

"No, you don't have to remind me of that," Casey finally said. "But the stability she needs comes from Blake, not me."

"I'm not so sure about that."

"If I didn't think leaving was the best thing for everyone, I wouldn't have come here and suggested it."

Ginger nodded thoughtfully. "I just hired someone to fill your previous position with the Redmonds. They're back from their extended vacation, and this seemed like a good time to make the transition since Heidi and Jack aren't used to seeing you every day."

Guilt flooded Casey when she thought about Mia's transition. The girl already had difficulty trusting, and Casey wondered if "Casey Thomas" would go on the list of people who had abandoned her. If only Casey's hormones didn't do a dance of joy every time Blake Decker walked into a room. That reaction showed no signs of letting up and the consequences of allowing the situation to continue could be bad.

No, leaving was the best thing for all of them.

"I'll look for a replacement," Ginger was saying. "But I don't know how long that will take. And I'd really rather not leave Blake in the lurch, without someone to supervise Mia."

"I understand," Casey said.

"So you're okay with hanging in there until I can replace you?"

"Yes."

Casey was surprised how okay she was with postponing her resignation. For one thing it would put off abandoning Mia and the guilt associated with doing that. She was carrying around enough guilt already and wasn't anxious to add to it.

It would also put off the moment when she had to say goodbye to Blake. The thought of not seeing him, not challenging him and, God help her, not kissing him filled her with a bleak, black sadness.

Had she always been this spineless? One minute convincing herself to leave and the next relieved she didn't have to?

Suddenly she could see the appeal of hiding in a cave.

Chapter Ten

"Uncle Blake said the party is really formal. Like the Academy Awards." Mia was quivering with excitement as she looked in the window of a dress shop displaying ball gowns.

"Yes, he did."

Casey smiled because this was the same mall where little Miss Decker had been caught shoplifting makeup, and that hostile, belligerent, abrasive and unpredictable girl was gone. Or at least taking a break. It made her, Casey, glad she'd agreed to suspend her age-limit rule. If she'd had even a small part in this change for the better, that made her proud.

It also didn't escape her notice that Ginger Davis lived just across the street, and Casey's most recent visit with her boss had been equally as traumatic as that first one with the Deckers, but for a completely different reason. When Ginger found her replacement, it wouldn't be easy to leave Mia.

And Blake.

That was exactly why she needed to get out as soon as possible. In the meantime Mia needed a dress and the nanny needed to provide guidance.

"Your grandparents' anniversary celebration is going to be in a banquet room at the Bellagio hotel."

Mia's eyes grew even bigger. "There's gambling at that hotel."

"Not where you'll be. All kinds of rules are in place to make sure of that."

"I know. But maybe I can peek." Her voice was a mixture of whiny and wistful as she stared into the display window. "With just the right dress, maybe they'd think I'm twenty-one."

Casey put her arm around the girl and eased her out of the flow of mall foot traffic. "Those look kind of grown-up for you."

"I don't want a baby dress."

"That's not what I'm suggesting."

"So I can get a strapless?" Hope gleamed in Mia's eyes.

"First you need something to hold it up." Casey glanced at the twelve-year-old's almost flat chest.

"I've got something. In fact, I've been meaning to talk to you about a bra."

It was on the tip of Casey's tongue to say she didn't need one yet, and especially not for a strapless dress. Two things stopped her. Mia looked completely intense and sincere. Casey knew from her own experience that teasing could be painful. When she'd gone through puberty and her body changed, there'd been no one to guide her. Her older brothers had made fun of her and her dad hadn't had a clue about girls. She'd muddled through on her own. Starting her period. Dealing with excess hormones and mood swings. Growing breasts.

She remembered the shock on Blake's face when he'd

seen the ugly healed wounds. Now her woman's body was scarred because an emotional tug for a kid had grown into seriously misplaced trust and then he'd used her for his violent ends. For the rest of her life, her body would bear the marks, and her heart the pain.

But for now her duty was to this girl. "We'll look for bras. There's a lingerie store here in Fashion Show Mall that advertises an expert in fitting."

"Really?" Mia asked, clearly surprised her request was being taken seriously.

"Really," Casey assured her. "You're twelve. Of course you need bras."

Mia grinned and started to clap her hands like a child, then stopped and looked around to make sure no one had seen her coolness factor slip.

"Wow, that was easier than I thought. Maybe now would be the time to say I'd also like a dress from this store." There was a longing expression on her face when she stared in the window.

"Let's go in and look. Maybe they've got something. But I have the final say. It's got to be age appropriate."

"For, say, a sixteen-year-old?"

"Don't push your luck, kid."

"But, Casey—"

"Have I ever told you that persistence is your least attractive characteristic?"

Mia laughed and slid her arm through Casey's, tugging her body forward and at the same time tugging on her heart. Casey's instinct was to pull back, but this child so rarely acted like a child—a normal, happy, carefree child. No way she'd do anything to stop that.

They walked inside and looked around at the dresses on display and the racks filled with fancy evening gowns. A very pretty saleswoman somewhere in her early twenties approached. Her layered brown hair teased her shoulders, and warm brown eyes welcomed them. "Hi. My name is Ava. Is this your first visit to Special Occasions?"

"Yes," Casey said. "Mia is going to her grandparents' anniversary party and needs a dress."

"Is it a formal event?"

"Very," Mia said. "But I don't want to look too—"

"Old," Casey interjected. "She's twelve going on twenty-five."

Ava studied the girl. "I have quite a few dresses that I think will work for your daughter."

"Oh, she's—"

Mia loudly cleared her throat. There was a gleam in her eyes that was all about teasing mischief. "She's such a *mom*. If a dress doesn't have a mile-wide skirt and pink ribbons, she thinks it's too old for me."

"And my *daughter* is trying to grow up too fast."

"Do you have any idea how many times I've heard this?" Ava smiled, then winked. "Trust me, Mia. I'll find something for you that both you and your mom will absolutely adore." The saleswoman studied Casey, then said, "I've got some fabulous dresses for you, too, Mom."

It took Casey a couple of beats to realize Ava meant her. "Oh, I don't need anything. I'm not—"

"Mom, you have to try on something. It will be a lot more fun if you do," Mia insisted.

Casey knew Mia meant attending the party, but debating in front of a stranger wasn't something she was prepared to do. "We're here for you, Mia. And I'm not much of a girlie girl."

"I can help you with that," Mia offered.

"My job is to help you both. And you've come to the right place," Ava said. "This is a full-service boutique—shoes, bags, makeup. We don't have a hair salon, but I can point you in the right direction."

"But I don't really need the full treatment," Casey said.

Ava held up a hand. "I find dresses. You try them on. If not one of them is something you absolutely must have, if they're not age appropriate, it will not hurt my feelings if you leave empty-handed. You have absolutely nothing to lose."

Casey looked at Mia, who had eagerness written all over her. "Okay, then."

It had started out as a way to make Mia feel more comfortable and escalated from there. Casey zipped and fastened dresses for the girl. They agreed that if the material and strings on a hanger needed a schematic to figure out which parts covered boobs and butt, it had to go on the reject pile.

When Mia tried on something she proclaimed a "Little Bo Peep on steroids" number, they laughed until tears streamed down their faces. Then she tried on a simple, light green, high-necked sleeveless dress that stopped at mid-calf. The color was perfect with her skin and eyes.

Casey stared and caught her breath, but she needed to tread carefully. "So, what do you think?"

"It's not horrible," Mia said cautiously.

"I agree."

"Do you think it's dressy enough?" the girl worried.

"The satin material makes it dramatic and elegant, I think."

Mia nodded as she stood on the round step in front of the full-length mirror and studied herself. "Does it make me look like I'm twelve?"

Casey sat in the chair and tapped a finger against her lips. "Better than that, it makes you look beautiful."

"Really?" Mia's eyes shone with pleasure. "You're not just saying that?"

"When have I ever said something just to make you feel better?" Casey said wryly.

"Good point." Mia looked back at her reflection. "But my hair—"

Casey stood and joined her on the raised area. She gathered the thick curls in her hand and piled the hair on Mia's head. "What if you have a French braid? Or do it up somehow?"

"At a salon?" Mia asked, incredulous. "That might cost a lot."

"As opposed to this dress, which is free?"

"Right."

"Look, kiddo, one of the first conversations I had with your uncle was about getting you whatever you need. And I think you need this dress and a visit to a salon. I've got the credit card, and frankly, this is a charge-worthy occasion."

"Shoes, too?"

"Absolutely." Impulsively the girl threw her arms around Casey and hugged her. Tears burned as Casey brushed a hand over Mia's thin back. "You're welcome."

"Now it's your turn," Mia reminded her. "There's one more dress in your fitting room. The royal blue one."

"I don't think it's worth the energy. Doesn't look like much on the hanger."

"But at least we know which side is front and which is back."

"That's because there is no back," Casey said.

"You don't have to buy it," Mia reminded her.

Finally Casey gave in, went to her fitting room and slid into the gown. The color was perfect for her eyes, and the high neck hid the scars, but the shimmery material clung to her hips and breasts, making her feel incredibly feminine and sexy.

"Come out and let me see," Mia begged through the door.

"Okay."

Mia gasped when the door was opened. "You look gorgeous."

Ava walked over just then and agreed. "It's like someone made that for you. And I'm not just saying that to make a sale."

If the criterion was that she had to have it, this was the one. "I don't know. It doesn't seem right to spend…" She remembered the ruse. "To spend your father's money on something this expensive."

"He said whatever I need," Mia reminded her.

"Your husband won't be able to take his eyes off you," Ava said.

Casey was never quite sure if that was what made up her mind or not, but she was going to the party in this dress. And she took Blake's credit card for quite a spin at Special Occasions. Makeup, silver sandals for both of them and evening bags added up fast. To ease the guilt, she promised herself that she'd pay Blake back. He could deduct some from her paycheck, although that would mean being in his employ for a good portion of the rest of her life.

As they left the store, she remembered what Ava had said. *You have absolutely nothing to lose.* And she realized the reality was that she had *everything* to lose. She was getting emotionally sucked in—by Mia and her uncle. And she couldn't even say for sure which one of them was the most dangerous.

In the banquet room at the Bellagio hotel his parents' party was winding down. Toasts had been made after dinner and now only hard-core partyers were left, small groups standing around chatting. Blake excused himself from several couples, longtime friends of his parents who seemed determined to bring up every stupid and humiliating incident of his youth. This was Lincoln and Patricia's anniversary celebration, not a Blake Decker roast. But he was taking the heat.

And speaking of heat…

In the subdued light of a chandelier on the other side of the room, he spotted Casey. He'd recognize her sexy back anywhere. When he'd first seen her and Mia with hair and makeup done and wearing formal dresses, he'd been in awe. He'd flat out said how lucky and proud he was to be escorting two such beautiful ladies.

Then Casey had turned, giving him an unrestricted view of her naked back—after which he'd been in serious danger of swallowing his tongue. The front of that dress said "sweet" and the other view was all about sin.

How weird was it that he was thinking about kissing every square inch of Casey's back, from the nape of her neck to the spot where her dress stopped, just above her butt? It probably wasn't completely weird, since he was a guy who seriously lacked a social life these days. Having these thoughts while Casey was talking to his mother was what bordered on weird. And then he realized that his mother was looking fairly intense about something, which cleared his mind of everything but the need to rescue Casey.

He made his way through the maze of white cloth-covered tables being cleared of dessert plates and after-dinner coffee cups. On some only the flower arrangements remained. Untouched flutes of Dom Pérignon for the earlier anniversary toast sat on a tray, and he grabbed up three when he walked by.

As he approached the two women, he heard his mother say, "I'm only thinking of you. There are no words to describe my gratitude to you for all you've done. This is a chance to know my daughter's daughter and I thank you for that."

"Hello, ladies." Blake's senses went on full alert with just a hint of scent from Casey's skin. "Champagne?"

"Thanks." Casey relieved him of one glass. It was a challenge not to stare at the way her royal blue dress clung to her firm breasts and the curves of her hips.

"I believe I will, too," his mother answered, looking just the tiniest bit guilty and uncomfortable. She was wearing a long-sleeved, floor-length black lace dress. Very elegant.

He raised his own glass. "In a less public way, let me say again, happy anniversary, Mother."

"Thank you, dear. Your toast earlier was lovely. As was your father's."

"So you're over being mad at Dad?"

"Not completely." Patricia sighed. "We've done more talking in the last few weeks than in the last forty years."

"Aren't you exaggerating?"

"Only a little. The bottom line is that he was wrong."

"But his heart was in the right place," Casey said. "He was trying to spare you more pain."

Patricia's gaze scanned the room and settled on a group of young girls and boys by the door. Mia seemed to be making friends with them. "She looks lovely with her hair done in that simple high ponytail. How did you manage to get her out of those scruffy jeans?"

"Two burly men and a muscle relaxer," Blake teased, meeting Casey's amused gaze. "Actually, that's a question for her nanny."

"Never underestimate the miracles wrought by the judicious use of a credit card," Casey said. "We found a great store and a fairy godmother, otherwise known as Ava, who made Mia over. I figured a little bit of makeup for this auspicious evening couldn't hurt."

Patricia nodded, a wistful sort of sadness in her eyes. "I've often wondered if we'd been more willing to bend with April, maybe she would have reached out for help."

"You loved your daughter and did what you thought best," Casey told her. "The only thing regrets accomplish is making you feel bad. It's a waste of energy that could be more productively channeled into your granddaughter."

"Very wise words for one so young, Casey." Patricia drank the rest of her champagne. "I'll do just that. Starting tonight. Mia is spending the night with us. She agreed to come home with Lincoln and me after the party."

"Really?" Blake glanced at Casey, who looked as surprised as he felt. "Did this miracle include the judicious use of a credit card?"

"No." His mother laughed. "I guess I caught her at a weak moment. Laura Parsons's granddaughter mentioned she was spending the night with her grandparents and I asked Mia if she'd like to do the same. Either she didn't want to turn me down at my party or she wanted to fit in with new acquaintances. Whatever the reason, I'll take it."

"Stroke of genius, Mother." Call him a selfish bastard, but he couldn't suppress the thought that he'd be alone with Casey. "And on the progress front, she's not calling you a dork anymore. At least not to your face."

"Woo hoo," Patricia answered.

Casey was just sipping champagne, and the unexpected comment made her laugh, then choke. He patted her bare back, wanting to help. Really. But the feel of her flesh beneath his fingers sent a burst of heat through him.

"Are you all right?" Patricia asked.

"Fine." Casey coughed again. "But next time I'd appreciate a warning when you plan to say something funny. Just a heads-up along the lines of 'Don't drink' before you cut loose."

"I would have if I had any idea I was funny." Patricia grinned at her. "You just made my evening. And now I think I'll begin what I hope will be a long and illustrious precedent of spoiling my granddaughter."

"Go, Patricia," Casey encouraged.

When they were alone, Blake looked down at her, trying not to be turned on by the way her hair was fluffed, as if a man had run his fingers through it during sex. "You're awfully chummy with my mother."

"Does that surprise you?"

"Since she's not the 'get chummy' type, I guess it does," he admitted. "She can be formidable. Distant."

"That's a defense mechanism. A facade. Clearly she's trying to change because she loves her family."

He watched his mother, who was talking and laughing with Mia and the group of young people. Maybe she was sincerely trying not to make the same mistakes. Or just being in grandmother mode. Her only responsibility was to love Mia and keep her safe. Either way it was a side to his mother that he'd never seen before.

And that made him remember what she'd said to Casey when he joined them—that she was only thinking of Casey. What was that about?

"You've certainly won over my mother. She obviously cares about you."

"I suppose." Casey smiled, but it was tense.

"What's wrong? Don't tell me nothing," he warned, on some level knowing she would.

"Do you really want to know?"

"I wouldn't have asked if I didn't." He set his flute of champagne on the table beside them.

Casey stared at him for several moments, then blew out a breath. "She cautioned me not to be getting monogrammed towels with your initials on them."

"What?"

"She called it the *Jane Eyre* syndrome," Casey explained. Fortunately she added more, because that made no sense. "Nanny falls for boss."

"She had no right to meddle—"

"I don't believe she was. In the most discreet way, she

warned me that your marriage didn't go well. I knew what she meant and told her you'd already mentioned the infidelity to me."

"Infidelity? What a delicate way of saying disaster," he commented.

"That's the same term your mother used." Casey met his gaze. "For what it's worth, Patricia would like to do bodily harm to the witch—although that's not her exact word. However, it rhymes."

"Go, Mom. I wonder how she'd do in prison."

"Never happen. A jury of her peers, mothers whose sons have been cheated on by their wives, would never convict her."

He shook his head. "I can't believe she talked to you about that."

Casey gripped her glass until her knuckles turned white. "For some reason she thought I should know that you really don't like to fail and wouldn't ever put yourself in a position to do it again."

Blake didn't know what to say to that. Patricia had never before interfered in his love life. That stopped him. Is that what this was with Casey? Two hot kisses and even hotter thoughts that were nowhere near in control? Had his mother seen something in the way he looked at Casey? Or the way she looked at him?

That sent the blood surging to points south of his belt. "I'll talk to her."

"No." Casey touched his arm and their gazes locked. Sparks seemed to fill the air and breathing was a challenge. When she pulled her hand away, it was shaking. "She means well."

"That's what you told her about my father. Apparently it's 'defend Lincoln and Patricia Decker' night."

"You might want to cut your parents some slack. It's their anniversary. A commemoration of a long relationship."

"And your point would be?" He knew she had one.

"Your mother was trying to explain what I already know. You're anti-relationship."

"She said that?"

"My words," she admitted. "I assured her I'd already noticed that your career is about extricating people from bad relationships. She was relieved to know that there's no danger of me expecting anything you're unable to give."

"I'm glad the two of you bonded over my disaster," he said sarcastically. "I get that I didn't put enough effort into the marriage. How did you put it? Oh, yes. I spent more time with my secretary than my wife."

"Blake, I didn't mean to—"

"Yes, you did. For the record, it takes two to make or break a marriage."

"I'm aware of that."

"Oh? You've been married?"

"Engaged," she said, shadows in her eyes. "But I found out it takes two and we weren't the right two." She set her glass on the table, beside his. "I'd hate if your mother's anniversary was spoiled. I'm asking you not to tell her that you know what she said."

Blake watched her walk away and suddenly wondered why Casey had related the conversation with his mother. Maybe to put up a barrier? Her own defense mechanism? To push him away? Did she feel she needed to do that after kissing him?

He couldn't blame her. A second or two longer both times and he'd have taken her and damned the consequences. He still wanted her; denying that would be a lie. In fact, he was more curious about her than ever, and all the warnings in the world couldn't make that stop.

He'd finally come to the conclusion that finding out everything about Casey was the only way to put his interest to rest.

Chapter Eleven

The last time Casey had so badly wanted a night to end, she'd been in a military hospital, her body battered, bleeding and burned. Tonight she was burning, but no one could see. Hopefully. She glanced at Blake, beside her in the elevator as they rode to the top floor of his building. Dark hair fell across his forehead, and stubble shadowed his cheeks and jaw, because his last shave had been hours ago. The effect seemed to make his already potently intoxicating eyes even bluer and so much more intense.

They said there was something about a man in uniform, and though Casey had worn one, too, she knew from frequent exposure that it was true. But Blake Decker in a tuxedo fell into a category all his own.

Sometime earlier the black tie had disappeared and the first button on his crisp white shirt had become undone, revealing just a glimpse of the masculine chest hair. It was enough to make her wish the shirt and jacket were gone. He could easily play movie hero James Bond. She was no martini, but that didn't mean she wasn't shaken and stirred. She was also incredibly grateful when the elevator doors opened and they were back in the penthouse.

She longed for the cool sanctuary of her room, because he was hot. Jalapeño pepper with habañero sauce hot. If she didn't get away from him soon, there was going to be an explosion of heat—and the collateral damage wouldn't be pretty.

Frankie padded into the entry to greet them, her paws clicking on the tile. Casey bent and gave the dog a hug, then laughed when she looked for Mia.

"Sorry, girlfriend, your buddy is doing some serious family bonding tonight."

"I thought she'd back out," Blake admitted, leaning a broad shoulder against the door.

Was he hoping she would? So he wouldn't be alone with Casey? And temptation? She was glad his mother had reminded her that Blake was anti-commitment. And she'd repeated it to him to make sure he knew that she knew that even Patricia was aware that he wouldn't do another relationship. Blake offered no future, and that should have put a stop to temptation, but it didn't even come close.

"I'm glad she went with your folks. This will be good for the three of them." And it would be best if she said good-night to Blake right now.

She scratched Frankie's head and the animal closed her eyes in doggy ecstasy. "Pete said he walked you, little girl, so we're in for the night."

"Would you like a nightcap?"

There was a seductive quality to his voice, making it deeper than usual. The timbre brushed over her nerve endings and thrummed them into vibration mode. A person didn't always know when she was at a crossroads, but Casey knew it now. She desperately wanted to accept his offer, but if she did, there was a very good chance the road would lead to his bed.

"Thanks, but…" She stood and met his gaze. "It's late. I'm tired."

"You're not the only one." He dragged his hand through his hair. "But I'm keyed up. If that makes any sense."

It did, because she felt the same way and was pretty sure she knew the reason. "Then a drink would probably relax you. I'll say good-night—"

"I hate to drink alone." The look in his eyes was one part teasing and two parts pleading, but completely irresistible.

It was hell when you came to a crossroads and took the wrong path, but her reserves of willpower were all used up. "Okay."

Blake shrugged out of his jacket and carelessly tossed it on the sofa in the family room on his way to the wet bar in the corner. He took two small snifters from a shelf, then poured an ounce of brandy into each.

After handing one over, he touched his glass to hers and said, "To sharing."

"You mean, to letting your folks get to know Mia."

Studying her over the rim of his glass, he took a sip. "No, I mean you."

"I don't understand."

"I hardly know anything about you, Casey."

"How long have I worked for you?" Her chest felt tight. "Do you have a problem with my job performance?"

"This isn't about the execution of your responsibilities. No one is questioning how well you've done your job. I want to know more about *you*."

"Like what?" As soon as the words popped out of her

mouth, she wanted them back. She knew what he was going to ask.

"How did you get those scars?"

She set her untouched drink on the edge of the wet bar. "That has no impact on my ability to interact with Mia."

"This isn't about my niece and you know it." He tossed back the rest of the liquor in his glass and set it beside hers.

"If it's not about Mia, then I've got nothing to say."

"This is one friend to another, because I think we've gone way beyond employer and employee. I've talked about my past. You made me face the fact that I didn't put as much effort into my marriage as I should have. Those were painful things I'd rather forget. And if anyone asks, I'll deny saying this, but it helped to talk about stuff. And I've liked spending time with you." Intensity burned in his eyes, a clue that he was remembering kissing her as much as referring to his own personal revelations. "I let you in, but you haven't returned the favor. I intend to change that."

"Or what?"

He shook his head. "I'm not going to fire you, if that's what you're implying. And I'm not letting you quit. Something happened to you and I think it would be good for you to talk about it. Let me be your friend, Casey."

It was his special brand of caring, which was half bullying and half kindness, that broke down her defenses. "It happened in Iraq…."

"I figured as much." When she didn't say more, he said with extraordinary gentleness, "Go on."

"There was this Iraqi kid. About fifteen years old. He started coming around when I was on patrol in Baghdad. My friend Paula—"

"A soldier?" he asked.

She nodded. "Corporal Paula Desiato. She wasn't in favor

of interacting with the people. She was skeptical because the good guys and bad guys have no uniforms to tell them apart."

"I see."

There was no way he could understand fear that never went away. Wondering if death was around the next corner, but having to round that corner, anyway, because it was part of the job. "This kid seemed sincerely sweet and every day we'd wave as the patrol went through town. Eventually I stopped to talk. He told me about his family and asked about mine. His father was a shopkeeper, and his mother a school-teacher. There were seven brothers and sisters. He wanted to know all about life in America. I showed him pictures and he shared his dream to someday visit New York. I was the one who let him get close. I didn't see the signs—"

He rubbed a hand over his face before asking, "What happened?"

"One day, when we stopped to talk, he blew himself up."

"Oh, God… Casey—"

She backed away when he reached for her. "It wouldn't have been so bad if I'd paid the ultimate price for being stupid and gullible."

"You paid a price. I saw the scars."

"Other soldiers besides me were hurt in the blast." She met his gaze as misery trickled through her. "I'm alive. Paula isn't. Her little boy and little girl don't have a mother, and I'm respon-sible. I went to see them and her husband after I got out of the hospital. He said they were doing okay. Couldn't have been more gracious. He tried to make me feel better, but nothing—"

Sobs she couldn't control choked off her words, and tears blurred her vision. If she'd been able to see, she'd have evaded Blake's arms, because she didn't deserve sympathy or comfort. But suddenly she was pressed against his solid, warm chest as he murmured soothing words she didn't really comprehend.

"I get it now," he said when she quieted.

"W-what?"

"Why you refused to take assignments with kids over ten."

"I can't ever bring Paula back, but I vowed to make a difference in kids' lives. I regret—"

"What was it you said to my mother tonight about regrets?"

He thought for a moment. "Oh, yeah. They only make you feel bad and are just a waste of energy. There was something else about channeling that energy. The thing is, Case, those aren't just words. You live that philosophy every day. You make a difference in kids' lives, too."

"In my opinion that's only possible before they're lost to outside influences. We have to get to them when they're young."

"And yet you've done wonders for Mia."

"Just lucky."

"Just you." He wrapped his arms more securely around her, his hands warm on her bare back.

Awareness seeped through her despair. The strong, steady beat of his heart seemed to pump life into her and suddenly just being in his arms wasn't enough. She lifted her head and met his gaze as something hot and hungry slid into his eyes. It would never be clear who moved first or whether by silent agreement they shifted at the same time, but in a heartbeat their lips touched.

In spite of their dammed-up feelings, the first contact was soft, sweet, seeking. He slid his fingers into her hair, cupped the back of her head to make the connection more complete. He took her top lip and sucked, sending a tingling heat exploding through her. The nibbling kisses he trailed over her nose, cheeks, jaw and neck were soft as fog, thrilling as lightning. When his hand moved to gently and tenderly cover her breast, the touch stole the air from her lungs, partly because she wasn't wearing a bra. He brushed his thumb over the silky material and her nipple hardened with the erotic attention. A muffled moan was clearly audible, but it was several moments before she realized that she'd made the sound.

When he lifted his head and looked into her eyes, Casey realized that his breathing was as erratic as her own. That only turned her on more. She lifted her hands with every intention of unbuttoning his shirt, the urge to touch his naked chest almost unbearable. But she realized there was something in her way.

She traced one of the fasteners and smiled. "I've never been accused of being the fashion police, but aren't these called studs?"

"They are."

His grin took the starch right out of her knees and she was grateful that his arm was still around her. "Oh, my."

"You probably shouldn't make any connection between this and—"

"You?"

He shrugged. "Yeah."

"Okay."

The single word chased the teasing from his expression, replacing it with need. He kissed her again, his tongue sliding into her mouth, taking and giving as heat built inside her and turned liquid. It coursed through her and made her thighs quiver as need pooled inside her.

"Blake, please—"

"Not here. I want you in my bed." The words were spoken against her lips, but when he lifted his head, his gaze challenged her, warned her that now was the time to say no if she wanted.

She wanted *him*. The "saying no" train had left the station when she'd agreed to a drink. When he held out his hand, she settled her fingers into his big palm. He led her down the hall, and it was probably the first time she'd ever thought this place was too big. It seemed forever until they entered his bedroom and she looked around.

The king-size bed butted up against a curved, carved headboard in heavy oak. Two matching nightstands stood on either side. A matching dresser and armoire took up space on the walls, with sliding glass doors in between that led onto the terrace. The curtains were open and lights from Las Vegas illuminated the room, including the tan comforter with black trim. *Very masculine. Very Blake,* she realized, looking up.

Standing beside the bed, he dropped her hand, then took off his shirt in a single fluid movement that didn't include removing the studs. He reached out and slid the top of her dress down, his eyes going dark and dangerous when he couldn't miss the fact that she was now naked from the waist up, too.

He cupped her breasts in his palms, brushing the puckered scars with his thumbs. "You're beautiful, Casey."

"No, I—"

"Trust me. Beauty is in the eye of the beholder. You're brave and beautiful. Take it from me."

"The beholder?" She wouldn't have believed it possible, but she smiled.

"Oh, yeah."

He bent to take first one, then the other nipple in his mouth, and electricity shot through her, straight to that most feminine place between her legs. She pressed her hands to his face and savored the rasp of his beard against her palms. When he straightened, she stood on tiptoe and kissed him.

"I want you, Blake. Now."

"Is that an order?"

"Does it have to be?"

"No."

Without answering, he reached over and threw the comforter and blanket down, revealing beige sheets beneath. In seconds he'd slid her dress and panties off and lifted her into his arms, settling her in the center of the bed. Before her mind had time to register the fact that the sheets were cold, he was beside her, naked and warm and strong. She felt his hardness pressing into her thigh as he pulled her into his arms, kissing her as if he were starving and she were an all-you-can-eat buffet.

He slid his hand over her belly and between her legs, slipping a finger into her waiting warmth. Brushing his thumb over the nub of nerve endings there, he rubbed and gently scraped until pleasure peaked and exploded through her. She came apart in his hands—but his arms held her together.

When the stars behind her eyes cleared, he reached into the nightstand and pulled out a square packet containing a condom, which he used to cover himself. He kissed her again, then nudged her legs open wider as he settled between them and with exquisite gentleness entered her.

Her breath caught as he filled her and her hips lifted to meet him. He thrust into her again and again and she found herself climbing that peak one more time. With one final push, he went still and groaned out his release as she held him as tightly as she could.

For a moment, he rested his forehead against hers, then left the bed. Some part of her pleasure-drenched mind registered the fact that a light went on and seconds later it was off, just before he rejoined her in the bed.

He gathered her to his side and she rested her head on his shoulder. "So—"

"I don't think I can move."

"Stay," he whispered.

And she did.

Casey woke the next morning to the smell of coffee. She opened her eyes and Blake was sitting on the bed—his bed, she realized. Still groggy, she sat up and the sheet fell away, revealing her breasts. Not too sleepy to be embarrassed, she pulled it up to cover herself, although that seemed silly since he'd kissed every square inch of her when making love to her.

Blake, on the other hand, was wearing black sweat shorts, a worn T-shirt and a sexy, self-satisfied smile that reminded her just how she'd managed to get herself in this predicament in the first place.

Good Lord, what had she done?

He handed her one of the steaming mugs. "Good morning."

"Is it?" She took a sip of coffee and realized it had cream and sweetener in it, just the way she liked it.

"What's wrong, Casey?"

So many things, so little time. But she figured it could never hurt to go with the obvious. "We had sex."

"Indeed we did." He didn't look the least bit concerned.

"We shouldn't have had sex," she pointed out.

"The last time I checked, two consenting adults were free to engage in intimate activities." One dark eyebrow rose. "I've been known to miss a woman's signals, but I don't think that's the case here."

Definitely not the case here. Her body was still humming from their intimate activity. If he wasn't her boss and she wasn't the nanny, she'd be in favor of another round of intimacy.

"No. I was more than willing," she said.

"Then I don't see the problem."

If that were true, nothing she said would make him understand. All she could do was damage control. There was a robe—his robe, because this was his room—on the bed, beside her. She set her coffee down on the nightstand and shrugged into the soft terry cloth as discreetly as possible.

"I need to take a shower."

"Casey, wait—"

"No. I have to go."

Blake rubbed a hand over the back of his neck. "We need to talk about this."

"There's nothing to say, except that it can't happen again."

"You think that will take care of everything? That just the words will make it all go away?"

"I hope so," she said. "That's all I've got. It was wrong and we both need to forget about it."

"Easier said than done. Casey, listen—"

"No. I have to go. Mia will be home soon."

He didn't try to stop her again when she hurried out of his room and to her own. After closing the door, she tossed the soft terry-cloth robe on her bed, the one that showed no signs of being slept in last night, because it hadn't been. She got in the shower and stood under the hot water for a long time, trying to wash away or reason through what had happened. Neither worked. She dressed, put on light makeup and fixed her hair. A last look in the mirror showed a woman who was still confused about feelings for her boss that just wouldn't leave her alone. Peeking into Mia's room, which was beside hers, she noticed that Frankie had been in there tossing around clothes and shoes. She'd missed her buddy last night.

Casey had missed her, too, and not just because nothing would have happened with Blake if she'd been there.

She was in the kitchen when the front door opened and the dog barked an enthusiastic welcome to Mia.

"Hi, you," Mia said. "Hello? Anyone home?"

Casey walked into the entryway. "Hey. Nice outfit."

Mia glanced at her too-big T-shirt and sweatpants. Her dress was on a hanger and covered by a garment bag. "My grandmother loaned me this stuff. She made me hang up my dress and put it in that thing."

"Did you have fun?" Blake asked as he joined them. He'd changed into khaki shorts and a powder blue shirt. His hair was wet from the shower.

Mia sat cross-legged on the marble tile and hugged her dog. The garment bag was on the floor beside her. "I watched a movie with them, and she made popcorn and hot chocolate and stuff. They dropped me off and said to tell you they'd call soon."

Casey refused to meet his gaze, because that would release a flood of guilt, something very distracting when struggling for normal was already a challenge. "Sounds very domestic."

"Whatever." Mia wrinkled her nose. "What did you guys do? Must have been pretty boring without me."

Casey met his gaze then and guilt flooded her, just as she'd figured it would. "We, um—"

"You're right, kiddo," Blake said, looking at his niece. "Boring. We just went to bed early."

Casey winced, even though it was the truth, because he didn't say they went to sleep. Being a silver-tongued legal eagle was a plus in this kind of situation. Twisting the truth was what he did.

But the explanation seemed to satisfy the girl, who barely reacted while she scratched Frankie's head. "Have you guys had breakfast? I'm starved."

"Your grandmother didn't feed you this morning?"

"All they had was gruel. I tried to be polite and eat it," Mia said, looking completely earnest. "But you could use that stuff to stick paper to the wall."

"It's oatmeal." Blake laughed. "And they're watching their cholesterol levels."

"Whatever." Mia's eyes sparkled with teasing mischief. "Until they get some kid-friendly food, I'm not going back."

"Cut them some slack," her uncle urged. "It was a spurof-the-moment decision to ask you to stay. They had no reason to think you'd take them up on the offer."

"Good point," she agreed.

"Give them a list next time, and I'd be willing to bet, they'd accommodate every last whim." He ruffled her loose hair and she jumped up and ducked away.

"I'll fix French toast," Casey offered. She needed to do something, anything, so that she was too busy to think.

"Sounds good." Mia started down the hall toward her room, while Frankie ran ahead of her in that direction.

"Don't forget to hang up your dress," Casey reminded her.

"Oh, right." Mia retraced her steps, bent and grabbed the dress, then was gone.

Casey headed back to the kitchen and started gathering the utensils and ingredients for breakfast. Blake joined her and poured himself a cup of coffee, then leaned back against the counter beside where she was working and doing her best to pretend he wasn't there.

"It's not a crime," he reminded her.

She didn't have to ask what "it" was, but refused to comment. After breaking eggs in a bowl and stirring in milk and cinnamon, she dipped thick slices of bread into the mixture, then set them in the preheated frying pan, where there was an instant sizzle. Three plates waited on the counter next to her.

Blake touched her arm. "The counselor says talking helps."

Before she could respond, there was a movement behind them, followed by the sound of Frankie's paws clicking on the tile floor. Casey looked past Blake and her heart caught.

Mia stood in the kitchen doorway, holding Casey's royal blue gown and one of the silver sandals that went with it. "Frankie found these. You forgot to hang up the dress."

The dog must have wandered into the master bedroom

and brought them to Mia. There was no reason to think the worst. *Just act normal,* Casey repeated to herself. "Thanks for the reminder."

"You left them in Uncle Blake's room." Mia's voice was filled with anger, disappointment and hurt. She glared at Casey and her uncle. "You had sex," she accused.

Blake set his mug down. "Look, Mia—"

"Don't lie to me, because I know you did," Mia interrupted. "Before she got sick, my mom always had guys coming over. Every time there was a new one, she ignored me."

"I'm sorry you had to go through that, Mia," he said quietly.

"Yeah, me, too." Her full mouth twisted bitterly as she looked at them. "And I'm sorry I'm in your way."

"That's not true," Casey protested.

"No? So it's just a coincidence that the first time I wasn't here, you guys hook up? I'm not a little kid. And I'm not stupid."

Casey set her spatula on the counter. "Of course you're not."

"My mom always said that if not for me she'd have had a life." Mia's words were more distressing for the void of emotion in her voice. "And I guess it runs in the family. I'm getting in your way, too, Uncle Blake."

"You're not in the way," he protested.

"Stop lying to me," she yelled. "I don't believe you. And I hate you both."

She threw the dress and the shoe on the floor, then turned and raced from the kitchen. Moments later the door to her room slammed shut.

It would have been quiet as a library if not for the sizzling French toast in the pan. The smell of burning drifted toward Casey and she turned off the heat.

Blake blew out a breath. "Should I talk to her?"

"Yes. But I doubt she'll open the door. You might want to give her time to calm down."

"I could use some, too," he admitted. "Then maybe I could come up with a closing argument, something really profound to make her understand."

Casey wanted to say good luck with that. How would a child make sense of it when the adults involved couldn't?

"Does she really hate me?" Blake looked bewildered. "I thought we were making progress. Was that my imagination?"

"No."

"I thought she missed her mom," he said.

"She does," Casey assured him.

"You wouldn't know it by what she just said."

"Try to see it from her perspective. Her mother repeatedly abandoned her when she was alive, and then she died, essentially abandoning her for good. She doesn't know how to handle the conflicting emotions of loving her mother, missing her and hating that she was always last on her mom's list." Casey understood two out of three from firsthand experience. "Lashing out is her way of dealing with it all."

"I don't know what to do with a little girl who's grieving for her mother, and at the same time resenting the way she was raised." Blake dragged his fingers through his hair. "Is she seriously screwed up? Maybe she wants to live somewhere else. Boarding school."

"The last thing she needs is to be dumped." Casey remembered that first meeting and how Mia had expected it.

The thing was, they had been making progress with her. Now things were back to square one. Actually they were further back than that and Casey blamed herself. It was her fault that another young life had just exploded right before her eyes. She'd failed another kid because she'd crossed a professional line with her boss.

She couldn't imagine how things could get worse.

Chapter Twelve

The next morning Casey rushed into the kitchen. "She's gone."

"Mia?"

Stupid question. Blake was looking at Casey, and his niece was the only other *she* in the house. His tie was hanging down the front of his gray dress shirt as he poured a quick cup of coffee before rushing to the office. He was late. Oversleeping was the price you paid when a certain sexy nanny kept you awake all night. On top of that, his niece was all screwed up and he didn't know how to fix it. Now Casey was telling him the kid was gone?

"I checked on her last night, before I went to sleep. I was worried because she didn't come out of her room all day."

"What happened?" he asked.

"She refused to unlock her door." Casey's forehead was creased with concern. "She wouldn't let me in. I figured she needed more time to, you know—"

Yeah. He knew. Deal with the fact that her guardian was getting it on with the nanny behind her back. He was no expert, but the way Mia had stared daggers at them yesterday, the rest of her life wouldn't be enough time to get over what she seemed to see as a betrayal.

He ran his fingers through hair still damp from his shower. He'd had no idea that his sister had put her own selfish needs above her own child's until Mia had angrily blurted out the truth yesterday. Apparently the inclination to indulge selfish needs ran in the family. Wasn't that what he'd done? In his own defense it had to be said that he was still new at this parenting thing.

Ditto on sex with Casey. It was great, although there was no such thing as bad sex. But with her it was different, somehow not just a release for the bottled-up need in his body. There was a relief that went clear to his soul—and he'd never considered himself a soul-deep sort of guy. He liked Casey. He liked her a lot and wanted to be with her again. The longing was like nothing he'd ever felt before.

But now he had a kid. He wasn't used to scheduling sex around kids' sleepovers, and having to clean up evidence of the intimacy, which would push buttons he didn't know Mia had.

He took a sip of coffee. "Did you look everywhere?"

"Yes, but feel free to look for yourself," she said. "She could be hiding under the bed, although her past history would suggest she's more of a flight risk."

"You think she ran away?"

"Yes. What worries me most is she didn't take Frankie."

Blake knew how much his niece loved the dog, and for some reason that worried him more. "How did she get out without Frankie letting us know?"

"I don't know, except Mia is good at running away."

Casey bit her top lip. "And she didn't take her cell phone. It's on her desk."

"Chances are she wouldn't answer even if we called," he said grimly.

"But she'd have it if she needed help. What are we going to do?" Casey was more than worried; she was scared.

"The last time she ran away, it was to my folks. If we're going by recent history, that's a good place to start."

"Of course." Hope edged out the fear in her eyes. "Call them."

"Already on it," he said, picking up the kitchen phone. After hitting speed dial, he waited impatiently while the phone rang.

"Hello?"

"Mother?"

"Blake?" There was a split second of silence before she said, "What's wrong?"

Odd. He'd never thought his mother knew him all that well to guess from a single word that he had a problem. Clearly he'd never given her enough credit. "Is Mia there with you and Dad?"

"I haven't seen her since yesterday morning, when we dropped her off." There was a mother lode of concern in the words. "If you have to ask, I assume she's not there and you don't know where she is."

"That pretty much sums it up," he admitted.

"What are you going to do to find my granddaughter?" she demanded.

He had to wing it, because there was no plan. He'd hoped there didn't have to be one. That Mia would be with his folks and finding her would be easy. And therein was his biggest problem with this whole thing. His focus had been on giving her a place to live while minimizing the inconvenience to himself. What that said about him wasn't pretty.

"Look, Mother, you and Dad stay put in case she shows up there."

"What are you going to do?" she asked again. "Contact the police?"

"It might be too early. But I know some people. I'll call them and maybe some strings can be pulled. The cops can keep their eyes open. We'll give them a description and what Mia's wearing."

"Don't let anything happen to her, Blake. That little girl has just come into our lives—" Her voice caught, which wasn't at all like Patricia Decker.

"I'll get her back, Mom. Don't worry."

"Like that will happen. I'm hanging up now so you can go find her."

He clicked off, then went to his study to look up the numbers for his Las Vegas Metro Police acquaintance. With Casey's help he gave the guy a description of the clothes Mia was last wearing, her age, height, weight and eye color. The guy promised to pass the word to patrol officers and detectives, all unofficially, and if there was news, he'd call.

"I can't do nothing." Casey paced in front of his desk. "I'm going to look for her myself."

"We'll take my car," he said. "I'll drive."

She met his gaze. "I thought you had a full schedule at the office."

"I'm canceling my appointments today." And tomorrow, if there was still no news.

"But it's awfully short notice."

"Stuff happens." He yanked off his tie. "People will just have to deal with it."

"Are you sure it's okay?"

He rounded his desk and stopped in front of her. Worry and dark circles turned her hazel eyes more green. He wanted to hold her and reassure her that everything would be all right. He wasn't sure about that, and holding her had gotten him into this mess, but he had to touch her. It was a mistake and he vowed the last one he would make, but he brushed his knuckles over the softness of her cheek.

"It's okay. I'm the boss."

"That's the rumor."

After calling his assistant, they hurried to the car and raced out of the complex, even though he had no idea where to look. Actually, that wasn't true. The mall was as good a place to start as any. They checked out Boca Park, which was the closest, without success. There were so many places a young girl could hide if she wanted. And he didn't even want to think about the predators who zeroed in on kids out in public. Mia was young and vulnerable, and he wished she'd taken Frankie with her. He'd never forgive himself if anything happened to her.

For hours they drove around, checking out shopping centers close by, then widening the search. Up and down streets, some upscale, others not so much. With every minute that ticked by, he grew more anxious, less hopeful. The apprehension in his mother's voice gnawed at him, along with her words about Mia just coming to them. There hadn't been enough time to really know her, and Blake hated himself for not even trying.

"Let's try that center on Charleston," Casey suggested. "It's not too far from downtown."

"Okay." Blake knew the way and took the on-ramp to Summerlin Parkway, then merged with the 95 South and headed to Charleston Boulevard.

The sun was going down and they were no closer to locating Mia. He glanced over at Casey. "What if we don't find her?"

"We will," she said. But the determination in her tone sounded forced.

"I'm not so sure. I don't think I ever realized before just how big the Las Vegas Valley really is. And she's just a little girl. It's getting dark."

"There are places to be safe."

"And just as many that are dangerous when the sun goes down. Her pattern might be running away, but being easily found was also part of it. This is different."

She looked over, her eyes huge and haunted in the muted light from the dashboard. "It just means that she's making a point."

As in teaching them a lesson. He prayed that a twelve-year-old girl didn't pay the biggest price of all for that lesson.

He was hoping Casey would disagree with him. He wanted her to say his idea was way out in left field and not even remotely possible. The fact that she didn't meant she agreed with him, and that ate away at his hope and cleared the way for fear to creep in.

"Anything could have happened to her," he said, forcing himself to concentrate on the road.

"There's no reason to go to a bad place." But she didn't look convinced.

"This is all my fault."

"You're good," she said. "But not all-powerful. That would make you God and your résumé doesn't include creating the world in six days."

If this were any other situation, her words would have made him smile, but not now. "We've talked a lot about patterns and mine is failing people."

"No, Blake."

"Want the list?" He glanced over to the passenger seat and saw that her gaze was on him. "I failed my wife. My sister. And I'm well on my way to failing her child."

"You took her in when she needed a place to go. You've given her family."

"Yeah. Some family."

"No one is perfect. The important thing is to try."

"That's my plan. If we find her."

"We will," she assured him.

"I'm going to hang on to that," he promised. "Everything you've said is right on."

"What do you mean?"

"You told me that we have no choice about getting involved with family."

"I remember."

"But there is one thing I *can* choose." He glanced over and saw the question in her eyes. "Mia wasn't the only one I let down by thinking only of myself. I let you down when I slept with you, Casey." She started to protest but he held up a hand. "It's the truth. I see that now. You pegged me right as an anti-relationship guy—a selfish guy. The thing is, I don't want to fail you, too."

"You weren't the only one who made the decision to be close," she whispered.

"I should have stopped it. Hell, I should never have started it." But he wouldn't say he was sorry it had happened. There was only so much he could take and he would never be sorry for having her just once. "Mia has to come first. It can't ever happen again, Casey."

After several moments she let out a sad sigh. "I know."

And he knew the emptiness of it would be his biggest regret for as long as he lived.

Blake had told her he was turning over a new leaf, and Casey soon had proof that it wasn't simply lip service. She'd suggested that she go with him to pick up Mia when the police called to say they had found her. He'd thanked Casey for the offer but said that his niece was his responsibility, which was good news.

And bad.

That left Casey alone in the penthouse. Not completely alone, since Frankie followed as she paced from the foyer to the family room. The dog looked anxious and confused. Casey almost smiled at the thought, because there was no overt change in the dog's expression, but somehow she knew Frankie was worried about Mia.

Casey had been worried about the girl, too, and about Blake. Pain and heartache followed when you let yourself care. And she did, about both of them, which was exactly what she'd feared would happen if she took this assignment.

Since she'd first arrived at One Queensridge Place, Casey had struggled to convince herself it was just another assignment, and had failed miserably. Lately it had begun to feel like a family—at least what she'd always imagined a family was like.

If she wasn't *already* in love with Blake Decker, Casey knew she was in serious danger of it.

But everything was different now because they'd been intimate. She still didn't know why he'd been the one to make her take that step. Since the IED—the improvised explosive device—had blown up her world and scarred her body, she hadn't slept with a man. More than one had tried, but no one else had touched her heart. That was more scary than a stroll through downtown Baghdad without body armor or a steel-reinforced vehicle.

It didn't take a battalion of shrinks to tell her she was feeling vulnerable. That had been clear since her first meeting with Blake and the resulting intense reaction to him. The question now was what to do about this job, since she'd compromised it.

Before she could wrestle with a course of action, Frankie barked and raced to the front door just before it opened. Casey heard Mia greeting her pet and hurried from the family room to the foyer. The girl was in the same jeans and green knit sweatshirt she'd been wearing the first time Casey had met her, the first time she'd run away. This made number three and they said the third time was the charm. Casey hoped that was true, because the too-risky behavior had to stop.

After a quick visual examination Casey determined that there were no bruises, scrapes, cuts or any outward evidence of trauma.

"Are you okay?" Casey's gaze jumped from uncle to niece and back again since the question was directed to both.

"She's fine." The look he settled on his niece was rife with anger. "She's also damn lucky."

"Why? What happened?"

"The cops picked her up in a particularly bad part of town with some particularly unsavory people who prostitute teenage girls."

"Oh, no. Did you..." Casey's heart squeezed tight. "Were they—"

"The cops got to her in time."

"Nothing happened," Mia said, hostility dripping from every word. Brushstrokes of boredom painted her face. But what she couldn't know was that the fear lingering in her eyes gave away the little girl still inside her. Or maybe she did know—because she buried her face in her dog's neck and held on tight.

Casey wanted to hug Mia close and two days ago would have without hesitating. But one night in Blake's bed had changed everything.

"We were worried about you," was all she said.

"Right." Mia looked up, then stood and folded her arms over her thin chest, hunched her shoulders forward.

Obviously her body language screamed self-protection, but was that because of what she'd experienced on the street? Because of figuring out what had happened between Casey and her uncle? Or because he'd already lectured her and levied consequences for her actions?

Casey decided to fish for clues. "So you guys had a chance to talk in the car on the way back from downtown?"

"Actually, there was no conversation at all," Blake said. "I was too angry and didn't want to say anything without thinking it through."

This was new. Until now he hadn't been emotionally invested enough to get mad. But Casey was concerned that waiting until tomorrow would mute the impact of anything he said and that they risked going back to business as usual.

"Is there something you want to say to Mia?" Casey asked, nudging him.

"Where do I start?" He ran his fingers through his hair.

Mia dropped to one knee again and put her arms around Frankie, who hadn't left her side. "There's nothing you can say that I want to hear."

"Tough." He put his hands on his hips. He was still in his black slacks and gray dress shirt, wrinkled now after hours of driving around, searching and worrying. His dark hair looked as if he'd run his fingers through it countless times and the shadow of his beard darkened his jaw. His eyes were shadowed, too, and had never looked more vividly blue than they did at this moment.

Casey's heart squeezed tight again, but it had nothing to do with anxiety or relief, and everything to do with an intense feeling of respect and caring.

"This has got to stop," he said.

"You got that right." Mia glared at him.

"What are you talking about?" He folded his arms over his chest when Mia pressed her lips tightly together and slid a glance in Casey's direction. The look said loud and clear what she thought should stop. And Blake didn't pretend to mistake it. "I'm the adult and this is my house. I set the rules."

"So it's a dictatorship?"

"Darn right," he agreed.

"You want me out of the way. I don't get what you're so mad about."

"You took off and put yourself at risk. Casey and I were worried. That's what I'm so mad about."

"You don't care about me," Mia accused.

"I don't *want* to care about you, kid. There's a difference."

Casey realized the words were brilliant, more so because the expression of concern and caring on his face underscored the message. He had protested the situation, tried his best to disconnect from this child who had nowhere else to go. In spite of everything, he *did* care. The best part was that Mia simply stared at him, without a bored, blistering or belligerent reply. He'd rendered her speechless.

"So, here's the deal. You're grounded—"

"I don't go anywhere, anyway," she said, suddenly finding words.

"No mall, movies or outings," he said.

"I'm a prisoner?" she wailed.

He thought for a moment, then nodded. "That works for me."

"This is stupid—"

He pointed at her. "Keep it up. I haven't handed down the length of the sentence yet. But every time you say something, it gets longer. And I haven't even started yet on taking away your phone and computer."

The girl opened her mouth, then shut it again.

Blake nodded with satisfaction. "Wise choice. The thing is, your behavior has got to change, Mia."

It was as if he'd been channeling her thoughts, Casey realized. This was a moment, a really good one.

He blew out a long breath. "I don't have all the answers and I'm winging it, because I've never raised a kid before. What you need to know is that taking advantage of the situation isn't an option for you. Not anymore. If you step out of line, there will be consequences. If you play by the rules, there will be rewards."

"I'm not a dog. That's what I do with Frankie," Mia protested.

"Is it working?" he challenged. Her silence spoke volumes and he nodded. "Running away has got to stop. It's another way of hiding. And it's dangerous."

"You can't tell me what to do—"

"Grounded for seven days," he said. "Maybe without TV. Care to go for two weeks?"

Mia sighed and tried to look bored and angry, but there were cracks in the facade. "No."

"Good answer." He tipped his head toward the hall. "Now go to bed."

Without another word Mia did as she was told, and Frankie followed. The door to her room closed quietly, which was a minor miracle. This was the first time that had ever happened after a confrontation.

Casey looked at him. "Awesome."

"You think?" One corner of his mouth curved up. "She scared the hell out of me, Case."

"Me, too."

He stared at her and she thought there was a yearning expression in his eyes. If anyone ever in the history of the world looked like they needed a hug, it was him. Casey was afraid that if she looked in the mirror, there would be a corresponding expression on her face, so she turned away.

And remembered what he'd said to Mia. Running away is hiding. How many times had she accused him of doing that? Did it take one to know one? Was she the queen of denial, putting rules on the age of the kids she cared for in order to hide from the mistakes she'd made?

"It's late, Blake. You should get some rest."

"Yeah." He hesitated and the air between them was charged. For a moment it seemed like he would say something personal. But he didn't. "See you in the morning."

Her heart cracked just a little more when he left her alone. Since she'd broken her rules on this job, the mistakes had gotten even bigger. What was up with that? She'd crossed a line and now she didn't know where her place was in this household. She still felt like the little girl who couldn't manage to fit in anywhere. She cared too much for Blake to be the nanny, but he'd told her they couldn't be more.

If it didn't feel so much like running away, she'd have given him her notice right then. But she didn't want to punish him for doing the correct thing. She was to blame for Mia's behavior, and he was absolutely right to keep his distance from her.

But why did the right thing have to hurt so very much?

Chapter Thirteen

"You didn't have to come with me to walk Frankie." Mia's voice was laced with resentment.

"I wanted to. The sun feels good." Casey strolled beside Mia on the condominium complex walking path, with Frankie taking the lead as opposed to taking off, which the dog would have done if she hadn't been on a leash.

"It's hot. You're only here because it's your job to guard me and make sure I don't run away again."

For the last week, during which the girl had been grounded, the two of them had spent a lot of time together, but awkwardness had been like a force field between them. Maybe it was time to get it out in the open, give Mia a chance to air her feelings.

"So, you haven't asked any questions about your uncle and me."

Mia lifted her shoulder in a "so what" gesture. "I don't have any."

"You're not a good liar, kiddo. And you're not in the way. That's the truth."

"Whatever." But Mia glanced over. "I don't believe you'd really answer me if I asked."

"Believe it." Casey's heart pounded but she tried to keep it from showing on her face.

"Okay." Mia stopped when Frankie sniffed a tree. "So what's between you and Uncle Blake?"

"Nothing." Without flinching, Casey met the girl's hostile gaze, because at this moment it was the truth.

"But there was something," Mia persisted.

How did she answer that when nothing about her and Blake was clear? *Keep it simple, stupid.* "What happened that night you were at your grandparents' was nothing more than a brain hiccup. For both of us."

"I don't know what that means." When the dog pulled at the leash, Mia started walking again.

"It means that now we have a respectful working relationship that's all about doing our best for you. Everything is back to normal." That part was a lie, but hopefully there was still enough little girl left in Mia to believe it was possible.

Casey hadn't had a mom to warn her that when a woman gave herself to a man, everything changed and it could never go back to the way it had been. She'd found that out for herself in high school—in the backseat of John Stratton's Camaro. It had been awful and there'd been no one to talk to. Pouring out the story to her dad and brothers had been out of the question, and she'd been too mortified to confess to her girlfriends. So she'd cried alone in her room and publicly pretended to be fine.

She couldn't even claim innocent ignorance for what had happened with Blake. She'd known if she took the step, everything would be different, but rational thought had been no match for the yearning to be in his arms.

It had happened. Now she had to deal with the collateral damage and hope that, at least for this at-risk child, things could go back to the way they were.

Mia mulled over the words for a while. "So you really are here to make sure I don't run?"

Inwardly Casey sighed with relief that the girl didn't seem in the mood for a cross-examination about her and Blake. They were now on to the topic that impacted Mia most— being grounded and losing her iPod.

"Actually, that's what being grounded for the last week is supposed to do."

"If I didn't walk Frankie, I wouldn't get any fresh air at all," Mia complained. "Kids need fresh air to grow and not get curvature of the spine and stuff."

Casey laughed. "That's a little melodramatic. Especially since house arrest is being lifted today. Your uncle is taking you out."

"Like I believe that."

Casey slid her hands into the pockets of her white cotton capris. "He said he'd be home early to pick you up for dinner and a movie."

"I repeat…like I believe that."

"I can see why you'd be skeptical. He doesn't have a perfect record, but he should get points for trying. Give him a break, Mia."

"Like he gave me?"

"You ran away. This restriction is about teaching you that certain behaviors are unacceptable. It's for your own good. Shows that he cares."

"He doesn't want to care about me," Mia reminded her.

Casey was pretty sure the girl understood what Blake had meant, but it was clear that she needed reassurance. "Not wanting to care is guyspeak for he doesn't want to, but against his will, he got sucked in and can't help caring."

Mia rolled her eyes. "I feel much better now."

"I'm serious. If he didn't care about you, no way he'd have gone to every mall in town, looking for you."

"He did?" Mia looked surprised.

"And you know how he feels about shopping," Casey added for emphasis. "He certainly wouldn't have grounded you for a week if he disliked you intensely."

"So you're saying house arrest is an awesome way for me to feel the love?"

Casey laughed. "Someday you'll understand that if he didn't care what happened to you, he wouldn't bother with restrictions. He'd let you do whatever the heck you want, because that would be much easier than putting up with your pity-party prison attitude."

Mia's mouth curved up, and for a split second it looked like a smile would break through the resistance. Then the crack in her facade disappeared. "Am I off suspension when he doesn't show up?"

"He will," Casey assured her.

"But if he doesn't, is the grounding up?"

"Yes." Casey sighed and hoped she wasn't wrong about him keeping his word.

He hadn't been faking the worry when Mia ran away. Casey had never seen him in action in a courtroom and some might say theatrics were part of pleading a case. But Blake's concern for his niece had been genuine. Would sincerity translate to keeping his promise now that the crisis had passed? Time would tell.

Casey looked at her wristwatch and saw that time was perilously close to running out.

They walked the dog back into the building and rode the elevator up to the penthouse. While Mia removed Frankie's leash and got her pet some food and water, Casey looked around in the usual places for the usual clues that Blake was home. She could have shouted, but in six thousand square feet it would have been a waste of breath. And speaking of a waste of breath, she didn't see his briefcase, suit jacket or anything else indicating that he was here.

"Can I have my iPod back now?" Mia asked, her resentful tone clearly indicating she'd come to the conclusion that she'd been stood up.

"Sure," Casey said. "But don't give up. He might still—"

The front door opened and Blake called out, "Sorry I'm late."

The dark shroud of bitterness lifted and Mia smiled. He walked into the family room and looked at Casey, then at his niece.

"You thought I wasn't going to make it," he accused.

"Never crossed my mind," the girl answered.

"You're lying." Blake grinned. "Should I be glad you're so bad at it?"

"Don't answer that, Mia," Casey advised. "It's a rhetorical question."

"I don't know what that means," the girl said.

"It's an attorney trick to trip someone up."

One raised eyebrow and a look from Blake said he could see that a week's worth of tension had eased. A teasing expression made his already handsome face even more appealing and Casey died a little inside.

"So, it's two against one," Blake accused. "In football they call that piling on. Unsportsmanlike conduct. That's a penalty."

"Not me," Mia said. "I'm officially not grounded anymore. This is me officially staying out of trouble."

"That's what I like to hear." Blake walked over and kissed her forehead. "Give me a minute to change clothes and we're outta here. The Deckers are going out on the town. Look out, Vegas. Here we come."

"Okay." The smile Mia gave him was heartbreaking in its hopefulness, a testament to how many times she'd been disappointed. But not this time. The little girl in her positively glowed.

When they were alone, Mia turned to her and said, "I didn't believe he would come for me."

"You were wrong."

"I know." She rubbed the spot on her forehead where he'd kissed her. "He really does care."

"I hate to say I told you so, but I told you so."

"I know." She grinned a very Decker-like grin. There was definitely a family resemblance. "Casey, I'm really, really sorry I was such a brat."

Would wonders never cease? An apology from the princess of pout. As Blake had pointed out, the lesson was learned and there was no point in piling on. "I've seen worse."

"You're just saying that to make me feel better." Mia caught her top lip between her teeth and worried it for a moment. "It's just that I was afraid."

"I know."

"I couldn't help it."

Casey knew that, too. "You're just being silly. Here with your uncle is where you belong. There's nothing to be afraid of."

"You're right. I'm just being an idiot. There's no reason to think that Uncle Blake loves you more, and now I'm sure that he doesn't. He and I are actual family."

Casey's mind filled in the rest. *And you're just the nanny. The hired help.*

Casey kept the carefree mask in place until the two of them left and she was alone. Suddenly her legs wouldn't hold her and she slowly sank to the carpet in the family room, which had never seemed quite so huge and empty before.

She felt as if she'd been slapped. Just because the slap had been delivered with words instead of an open palm didn't make the message less powerful.

Or hurtful.

She knew Mia hadn't meant to wound her, but the arrow had hit its mark with deadly accuracy. The kid was beginning to realize where she belonged and to feel secure enough to say so. Casey envied the twelve-year-old and wished it were possible for her to know what that felt like just once in her life.

Since sleeping with Blake, she'd been caught in an alternate universe: she was neither a paid professional nor his plus one. A verbal slap was just what she'd needed to snap her out of it. Even though he'd made it clear that Mia was his priority, and rightfully so, Casey hadn't quite been able to crush out the hope that she had a ghost of a chance with him.

But Mia had just taken care of that. There was no future here with the Deckers, and the sooner she left, the better off everyone would be.

Blake tried to focus attention on his computer screen, without much success. Something was bugging him and he couldn't quite put his finger on what it was. He leaned back in his chair and glanced at the picture of Mia on his desk. It had been taken a few days ago, on her first day of school—middle school. Before long she'd be in high school, then college. Then what?

Oddly enough he didn't much like the idea of her being somewhere where he couldn't make sure she was okay. That day of worrying about her out in the world alone, of picturing all the bad things that could happen, had made him want to put off her independence as long as possible. The day was coming when she'd push for it, but that wasn't today.

The door to his office opened and Rita poked her head in. His administrative assistant was an attractive woman in her mid-forties with brown eyes and shoulder-length black hair cut in layers.

She put a stack of papers on the desk in front of him. "I've got correspondence ready for your signature."

"Thanks, Ree."

"Cute kid," she said, looking at the photo.

"My niece. Mia."

"I see the family resemblance. There's something stubborn about the tilt to her chin, the determination in the eyes." She put the frame down. "A word of warning?"

"Shoot."

"Exactly." She nodded emphatically. "When boys start showing an interest, make sure they know you have guns and know how to use them."

"I'd be lying."

"Bluff. You're good at that. They'll never know for sure and will be inclined to keep their distance from that sweet little girl."

"Okay. I'll take that under advisement."

After his assistant left, his gaze wandered to the photo and he straightened it on his desk. *A sweet little girl.* He remembered the first few weeks she'd lived with him and the attitude she'd worn like armor. He hadn't known how to strip it away. If not for Casey...

He was pretty sure these last couple of months of adjusting to having a kid around would have been impossible without Casey. Too many times recently he'd had the uncomfortable feeling that life would be impossible without her. The tight feeling in his chest made him frown, because just thinking about her made him want to hold her. It seemed like a lifetime ago when he'd made love to her.

Except he knew his thing for Casey wasn't just about sex. That was pretty awesome. But even that word didn't do justice to the experience of holding her soft curves against him, kissing her sweet lips, loving her until he thought the top of his head would explode.

Bad analogy, he thought, remembering the scars on her body from the explosion, for which she blamed herself. He had a feeling that the wounds she carried on the inside were far worse than the ones he could see. He'd read about it: PTSD, post-traumatic stress disorder.

Casey Thomas was a complicated woman and he couldn't stop thinking about her. The intense feelings shook him up. They were deeper and more compelling than what he'd felt for the woman he'd married, the same one who'd betrayed and blindsided him. He'd never expected the bad stuff, and now he couldn't picture himself expecting anything else. A shrink would probably tell him what he already knew—he had his own emotional brand of PTSD going on.

He needed breathing room. He needed—

The intercom buzzed and he pushed the button. "What is it, Ree?"

"Casey Thomas is here to see you, Mr. Decker. She says she's your nanny."

His heart thumped once and he took a deep breath before answering. "Send her in."

Moments later there was a soft knock on his door before it opened and she was there. "Hi."

Her smile released the full power of her dimples, which, he'd found out for himself, were her secret weapon. When they flashed, mass destruction followed, because men would fall at her feet. At least he had. The memory was like a blast of heat that went from brain to gut to groin—the trifecta of turn-on.

"Hey. Come in." It was a major effort to keep his voice

normal, and he wasn't sure he'd pulled it off when she looked uneasy.

That made two of them, he thought, noting the way her white cotton sundress pulled across her breasts. All the skin he could see was tanned and toned, and the toes peeking out of her flip-flops were painted pink. She moved farther into the room, and he held out his hand, indicating the two club chairs in front of his desk. She sat in the one on the right and set her purse in her lap.

He shifted in his chair and sat up straighter, grateful that his desk was between them. That made him realize something else. This was the first time she'd come to see him at the office.

"Is everything all right?" he asked. "Mia?"

"Fine. I just dropped her off at school."

"How's that going?" He was grateful for a topic to take his mind off the disturbing thoughts of him, her, twisted sheets and tangled legs.

"It's the first week, but so far so good."

"By good, do you mean that there have been no phone calls from teachers or the administration?"

"There's that. But I mean she's talking about kids and classes and activities." Casey smiled and the dimples danced.

His gut knotted at the sight, and he wondered if there was a topic of discussion known to man that wouldn't make him think about having her in his bed.

"Good. I'm glad to hear it."

She frowned. "Are you okay?"

Not really. This was nice. Too nice. Distracting, but nice. That meant there were fewer hours until it would be time to go home, where Casey would be waiting for him.

No. Scratch that. She'll be there supervising Mia. Doing her job. That's all. He needed breathing room.

"I'm fine." *Mostly.* "Happy to hear that Mia is settling into school."

"Yeah. She likes the teachers. By the way, she wants to go to the new restaurant at Encore when you have your next Deckers' night out."

He laughed, which was hard to believe. "She's been a different kid since I grounded her."

Shadows filled her eyes for a moment, before she said, "The transformation has more to do with you showing up for dinner and a movie than with punishment for bad behavior. Setting the parameters and sticking to them are the cornerstones of positive parenting."

"I enjoy spending time with her," he said, surprised he hadn't actually thought in those terms until this moment. "She's fun, funny, smart. She's really a great kid when she's not acting bitter and resentful."

"You pretty much described every kid in the world," Casey pointed out.

"Yeah." He leaned back in his chair. "But in Mia's case it feels like a miracle when I think about how she was at first. She's great to have around and that's something I never thought I'd say."

"You should tell her that."

"Good idea. Which reminds me that I have you to thank for the sheer normalness of her behavior."

"It's nothing."

"Not from my perspective," he said. "Your work with Mia has been exemplary. And to show my gratitude, there will be a bonus in your paycheck."

He was looking straight at her and would swear her face didn't alter, but suddenly it dimmed, as if clouds had blocked out the sun. And since when did he analyze the facial expressions of his employees? Since things took a personal turn, and that was as good an example as any of why he needed to put things back on a firmly professional footing.

"So, what brings you here? I'm guessing it's not about updating me on Mia's first week of school."

"No." She gripped her purse tightly. "I'm handing in my resignation."

That wasn't what he'd expected. "You're quitting?"

"This is my two weeks' notice."

"I don't understand," he said.

"It's my intention not to work for you any longer and I'm notifying you of that."

"That's not what I meant. I get what *resignation* means. It's just that I thought taking care of Mia agreed with you."

"As you said, she's a great kid. I stopped by your office because this isn't something I wanted her to overhear."

His first thought had been about himself, about how much he'd miss her. But Casey was worried about how Mia would react. No one liked change, but a kid who'd been through what she had would take it especially hard.

"She's doing so well. I'd like to see her continue with the forward progress. All those rough edges she had when she first came to live with me have been smoothed out."

"I'm glad. But this is about me. I've got rough edges, too, and they're not smoothing out."

Her eyes said she was dead serious and told him change was in his future. Mia wasn't the only one who didn't like change. "Why, Casey? You're part of the family."

"How exactly?"

"What?"

"How am I part of your family?"

Blake thought about the question. "You take care of Mia."

"Last time I checked, child caregiver wasn't an official limb on the family tree."

"It's the only answer I have," he said.

"Not the one I was hoping for." Her voice was soft and sad. Her smile was sadder and even the flash of dimples didn't restore the sparkle.

Blake realized that this was what had been bugging him, keeping him from concentrating on work. Casey hadn't been acting like herself for about a week, since just about the time Mia got off restriction. Just about the time things with his niece had clicked into place. Personally? He hated the idea of Casey not being there, but that wasn't something he wanted to think about now.

"Is it about money? I'll give you a raise—"

"No. I have nothing more to say." She stood and slid the strap of her purse on her shoulder.

He stood, too, but didn't dare walk around the desk, because he would have pulled her into his arms. "Casey, wait—"

"It's no use, Blake. There's nothing you can say that will change my mind."

"Why are you so determined?"

"You know why." She sighed. "What happened between you and me was an error in judgment."

An understatement, and yet he couldn't regret what had happened. "It's in the past. We can—"

"No. It's not possible to forget. With me there Mia has to try too hard. That will make it much more difficult for the two of you to form a family unit." She met his gaze and determination filled her own. "My bad judgment tore apart the family of my best friend. If I can heal yours, maybe that will make up for it in some small way."

He didn't say anything else to try and stop her. Partly because the knot forming in his chest was cutting off his air, and partly because there was nothing left to say. If he told her he had feelings for her, she wouldn't believe him. Trust was a problem, and she'd think he was using her, like she'd been used once before.

The feelings of anger and loss raging through him were a lot like what had happened when he'd found out his wife was cheating on him. But Casey hadn't betrayed him. She was straightforward, honest and had more integrity than anyone he'd ever met. Case in point: she'd come to his place of business and told him to his face that she was leaving his employ. And why.

Somehow that just made him feel worse.

Chapter Fourteen

As it turned out, Casey didn't stay for two weeks. Since Mia had started school, she only needed someone at home until Blake returned from work. With that parameter Ginger Davis had easily found a replacement.

He looked in the mirror and concentrated on shaving, because that was something he could control. And it was important to get a handle on something when it felt like his personal life was in free fall. Make that free fall minus one.

Mia was doing great. She'd taken the news of the shift change surprisingly well. Actually she'd shown very little emotion when Casey broke the news. With the mature woman who made sure Mia made it home, started her homework and didn't have wild parties or watch inappropriate movies on TV, the kid's life was very much together.

"One out of two Deckers is still fifty percent," he said to his reflection. He grabbed a towel and wiped traces of shaving cream from his face before shaking his head at the sad-eyed fool looking back. "Pathetic loser."

With a towel around his waist he walked past the bed. His chest felt tight as memories of lying there with Casey washed over him. They'd been as close as a man and woman could be, sharing their bodies and bits of their souls. Since she had gone and no longer shared a part of his space, even time with Mia had been lonely and empty.

"Damn." He clenched his fingers into his palm, wanting to put his fist through a wall as angry frustration expanded inside him.

Deliberately turning his back on the bed, he walked into the closet and pulled out a black suit, a charcoal shirt and a gray-on-gray silk tie. The professional business attire was somber and funeral-like, which was appropriate since he couldn't shake the feeling that someone he cared very much about was lost to him.

There was a knock on the bedroom door, followed by Mia's voice. "Uncle Blake?"

"Just a minute," he called out. What was her problem?

He pulled on boxers, slacks and the shirt, buttoning it as he walked to the door and opened up. "Why aren't you on your way to school?"

"I missed the bus." Wide and not-so-innocent eyes stared back at him.

"Darn it, Mia. You had plenty of time. I'm running late for court."

"I could stay home from school today," she offered.

"No. Why did you miss the bus?" he asked.

"I had to come back."

"What for?" he demanded.

"I had a paper. But when I came back, Frankie—"

He held up a hand to stop her. "Don't even tell me the dog ate your homework."

"Why not?" Mia held up tattered sheets of notebook paper. "She ate your computer."

The one he'd forgotten to close up because thoughts of Casey had pushed everything else out of his mind. "Don't blame the dog. You're the one who's supposed to put things where she can't get at them."

"It's not my fault," she protested. "The new chick put my stuff in the wrong place."

"Her name is Barbara and I'm not sure that having your things in a different spot is an adequate defense."

"Whatever."

There was a word he hadn't heard in a while. "Is that kid-speak for, 'you didn't look for your backpack, to put your homework in it'?"

"It took me too long to find my school shirt. Friday is spirit day and we have to wear the one with the school logo. If Casey was here, it would have been where I could find it."

If Casey were here, a lot of things would be better, but that ship had sailed. "Then from now on we'll have to make sure everything is together the night before."

"I'm hungry." Her voice was just this side of a whine, which grated on his last nerve.

"Did you eat breakfast?"

"There's nothing good."

"You better be wrong. I pay a housekeeper a lot of money to stock the pantry and prepare meals."

"There's just cereal." She heaved a huge, long-suffering sigh. "When Casey was here, she made me eggs and Mickey Mouse pancakes with chocolate chips for eyes and a mouth."

Blake glanced at the clock and struggled for patience. "How about we make some of those tomorrow? It's the weekend and it'll be a fun thing to do together."

Mia nodded but was still making a frowny face. "But I'm still hungry now."

He knew she was being deliberately difficult, and wanted to shake her. Casey would have told him that rattling his cage was Mia's endgame and not to fall for it. He was doing his best, but the strategy would have been easier to stick to if Casey was here for backup. He felt as if he were walking a tightrope over the Grand Canyon and working without a net.

"Why don't you make yourself a peanut butter sandwich? You can eat it in the car on the way to school."

"Eat in the Benz?" she said. "Since when?"

"Since you need a ride to school."

"I thought you didn't have time."

"I don't," he agreed. "But you have to get to school. I'll work it out."

"You wouldn't have to if Casey was here—"

"But Casey isn't here." Blake's voice was louder than he'd intended and Mia's eyes grew wider as she backed up a step.

Blake looked down as he put his hands on his hips. He blew out a long breath, and when the haze of annoyance-fueled anger disappeared, there was a glimmer of understanding in its place. He looked at the girl, who was nervously biting the inside of her bottom lip.

"Look, Mia…" He tried to picture Casey dealing with this situation. There would be honesty, tough love and a little humor tossed in to take the sting out of it. "I'm sorry I yelled at you, even though you deserved it."

"Me?" She pressed a palm to her thin chest. "I forgot stuff. Do you want me to get a zero for homework? It was an honest mistake and you're acting like I did drugs or had sex."

He wanted to recoil in horror at the words but held tough because Casey had taught him not to react to the kid's tactics. "You're smart and capable and organized."

"No, I'm not."

"Look, kid, I'm an attorney. Last time I checked, stupidity wasn't a legal defense. You know better. And both of us are aware that you know better. I'm not as dense as you think."

"Oh, yeah?"

He had her on the run. It was time to get to the heart of what was really going on here. "This is about something else that's out of your control, isn't it?"

"That's just stupid."

Translation: he was on the right track. "No, it's not. You miss Casey, don't you?"

It wasn't so much that he was a mind reader or even an especially intuitive guy. He knew because he missed Casey, too. Her absence left an all-encompassing emptiness, which just couldn't be filled with work or parenting or even the general business of life.

Mia stared at him with a resentment he hadn't seen for a while, but now it didn't work. Full lips trembled as her big turquoise eyes filled with tears. "Why did she leave us?"

Blake pulled her into his arms and murmured reassuring words as he rubbed her back. "I know how you feel."

With her cheek on his chest, Mia nodded. Fortunately she didn't ask how he knew, because he'd have to be honest and he couldn't go there now. The girl's arms slid around his waist and that felt pretty good. It was the only thing about this day that did. When she stopped crying and stepped away, she rubbed a finger beneath her nose.

"Why did you let her go, Uncle Blake?"

"I didn't *let* her. She quit."

"Why?"

"She thinks you and I are having trouble being a family. She didn't want to get in the way of that."

Mia's red-rimmed eyes looked troubled. "Why would she think that?"

"It's complicated," he finally said.

She sniffled. "I told her I was sorry for being a brat."

"It's not your fault." She nodded, but he could tell she didn't quite believe the words. "Now, go make your sandwich and I'll drive you to school."

Without another word, she turned and headed toward the kitchen. Blake finished dressing.

No one was at fault for what had happened except him. He'd finally found a woman who was more interesting to him than anything, someone worth leaving work for, the one who was waiting for him to come home. And he realized the truth: he was in love with Casey and had pushed her away. Some misguided sense of guilt about Mia had convinced him he had to choose. But his niece's behavior just now convinced him that she loved Casey, too.

And he'd let her go.

If he'd told her how he felt that day in his office, there might have been a chance for them. But now she wouldn't believe him; she would think he was using her for Mia, for his own selfish purpose. He'd never be able to convince her that he needed *her.* From the beginning, the one thing they'd agreed on was that trust was hard to come by.

That fact didn't inspire confidence in his ability to get her to believe he was no longer anti-relationship.

Blake's career choice involved keeping his cool when the people around him were losing theirs. Since Mia had come to live with him, his emotions had been on a roller coaster, and he wasn't sure why he'd expected today to be any different. But he had and it wasn't.

He'd gotten a call from Mia's new nanny, who was freaking out because the kid hadn't come home from school on the bus. He had figured out she was upset about losing Casey, but had underestimated her emotions yet again.

He'd been canceling the rest of his appointments for the day when Ginger Davis had called to let him know Mia was with her. Now he was on his way up to her penthouse across the street from Fashion Show Mall. This felt a lot like coming full circle, except for the fact that Casey wouldn't be there.

After ringing the bell, he waited just a moment before Ginger opened the door. As always she looked stylish in a deep olive-green-colored crepe pantsuit.

"Hello, Mr. Decker," she said. "Please come in."

"Thanks. Where's Mia?"

"In my office." When he started to walk past her, she put a hand on his arm. "Don't be too hard on her."

"Give me one good reason why I shouldn't ground her until she's thirty-five."

"For one thing you'd never make that penalty stick." She smiled. "And you need to know that she came to me because she wants to see Casey and figured I would know how to find her."

"Do you?"

"Yes."

"Then tell me where she is," he wanted to say. But he didn't. Casey had turned her back on Mia and him. "I'm aware that Mia misses Casey very much. But I had no idea she would do a disappearing act yet again. There have to be consequences."

"And rightly so," Ginger agreed. "I just think you should listen to her before handing down a harsh sentence."

He was feeling pretty raw right now and the kid wasn't the only reason for it. "I'll take it under advisement."

Ginger nodded. "Follow me."

She led him to her office, a very female space, with its

glass-topped desk, pale yellow walls and floral print-covered love seat.

Mia stood when she saw him. "Uncle Blake, I—"

He pointed at her. "You're in so much trouble, young lady."

"I know. It's just that I had to do something."

"Do you have any idea how frantic I've been since Barbara called?" He studied the contrite expression on his niece's freckled face, and somewhere in his anger-drenched mind, it registered as sincere. "You're grounded from all electronic devices you now own and any that you ever hope to have in the future."

"Okay."

"Okay? No argument?" He hadn't expected it to be that easy.

"I deserve it." She folded her arms at her waist, as if she were hugging herself. "I knew you'd be mad, but it was a chance I had to take. I need to talk to Casey."

"Why?" he asked. "What's so important that it is worth losing your gadgets for the rest of your life?"

"It's my fault Casey left."

"What? Why?"

"I was mean to her," Mia confessed.

There had to be more. Casey had been a soldier, trained to take orders even when no one said please. Obviously she was sensitive, the most caring person he'd ever known. But she wasn't thin-skinned when it came to dealing with kids.

"Tell me what happened," he suggested.

"It was the night you came home from work to take me to dinner and a movie after my punishment was lifted." Mia glanced up at him without quite meeting his gaze. "I—I didn't think you'd keep your promise."

Yeah, he deserved that. "Go on."

"I'm not trying to hurt your feelings, but it's the way things were." It was good she'd used the past tense. "I was so happy to see you and I might have said that you didn't care about her."

Might have?

"What did you tell her exactly, Mia?" Ginger asked.

The kid glanced at Ginger, who was sitting behind her desk. "I was afraid Uncle Blake loved her more. I—I said something about her not being family. Not like he and I are family."

"I see." Ginger's tone was quiet, nonjudgmental.

Blake felt like he was suddenly groping his way around, because his vision was fuzzy. "Why would you say something like that to her?"

"I don't know. It's just…" She looked sad and miserable. "I wanted you to love me."

The words were like a punch to the chest and he pulled the girl into his arms. "I do love you, Mia," he said quietly.

"I know. And I'm sorry about coming here without saying anything, but I just wanted to tell Casey that I'm sorry."

"Your heart is in the right place, kid. It's your communication skills we have to work on."

"Yeah." She giggled and nodded.

"Mia," Ginger said, "would you mind waiting in the other room while I speak with your uncle?"

"Sure." Mia looked up at him. "Is that okay?"

"Sure." He kissed the top of her head. "I worry because I love you. I've had my quota of worry for one day, so I'd appreciate it if you didn't take off, like the last time we were here."

"I can do that if you'll let me keep just my iPod while I'm grounded."

"No." He grinned. "But that was a nice try. You've got some negotiation skills going on."

"It was worth a shot, but I wouldn't run away. I'm not that stupid kid anymore."

"Darn right. You're my kid," he said.

"I love you, Uncle Blake."

The words left him with a lump in his throat, so he touched his heart and pointed at her. She smiled, then said, "Maybe you can talk Miss Davis into telling us where Casey is."

"Are you going to ground her?" Ginger asked after the girl had left the room.

"I'll probably give her a suspended sentence." He turned to look at her. "I wonder if Casey has any idea how much she's hurt Mia."

"Mia? Or you?"

"That's ridiculous." But the words had struck a chord somewhere in the region of his heart.

Ginger folded her hands and rested them on her desk. "I think you're in love with Casey."

"I'm nothing more than the guy who signed her paycheck," he said, wincing at the bitterness in his voice, even though he'd already figured that out. "Have you talked to Casey?"

"Yes."

"How is she?" He wanted her to be fine and not fine. He wanted to know that she missed him the same way he missed her.

"She's doing as well as can be expected," Ginger answered cautiously.

All he heard was that she was doing well and something twisted in his chest. "That's because she's the one who walked away."

"Casey cares deeply about you."

He met her gaze and knew the cynicism in his soul showed in his expression. "That's hard to believe. You don't run away from the ones you love."

"Do you know what happened to Casey when she was overseas?" she asked.

"Yes."

"She had two reasons for walking out on you, Blake. The first concerns the trauma she experienced. You know that she saw her friends blown apart. And she believes it was her fault. Because she took an interest in a kid who used her."

"She told me," he said.

"Then you also know that her best friend's death left two small children motherless and that Casey blames herself for tearing that family apart."

"Yeah."

"Do you get that she won't be responsible for ruining another family? One that's just getting on its feet?"

"But she brought us together," he protested. "If not for her, we would be strangers living under the same roof."

"Did you tell her that?"

"I tried, but—"

"That brings me to the second reason," Ginger said. "She won't be made a fool of."

"I wouldn't do that."

"Not on purpose." Ginger picked up a pen and rolled it between her fingers. "But she let someone in once and it cost her plenty. I will not let you call her a coward. She's an extraordinarily courageous woman who would sacrifice herself for the ones she loves. Walking away from you and Mia was her doing that. She would give up her life, but risking her heart is so much harder."

"You think it's easy for me?"

He remembered what Casey had said about his career revolving around destroying relationships. His law practice had actually become more successful following his own divorce, and now he knew that was a result of channeling his bitterness into his business. He was a hotshot attorney who thrived on being alone, but after Casey all he had was loneliness. He could feel himself withering. Suddenly he was tired, weary clear to his soul. And he didn't want to be alone.

"I would never deliberately hurt her," he said. "But I don't know if I can convince her of that."

"Did you make an attempt?" Ginger's expression was kind, sympathetic, and it was as if she'd read his mind. "There's no shame in failing, Blake. Only in failing to try."

"She's not the only one with baggage," he pointed out. "And I'm not accustomed to losing."

"You don't have to be perfect. You just have to show up and do your best."

She made it sound easy and he knew it wouldn't be. But he also knew that if he turned his back now, it would be the biggest mistake of his life.

"Do you know where she is?" When Ginger nodded, he asked, "Will you tell me?"

"She requested that I not *say*."

Blake hadn't become a successful attorney by not paying attention to the fine distinctions of words. His heart picked up speed when she reached for a notepad and jotted something down.

"This is me not *saying* where she is." Ginger slid a piece of paper across the desk.

"Thank you." He met her gaze. "I'm not sure how to do this."

"You've been hurt, too, Blake, so it's not easy to take a chance. But I just saw how easily you told Mia what's in your heart. And I know there's a different sort of risk with Casey, but just tell her what you feel."

Blake nodded as he took the address from her. He knew he was good with words and had delivered successful summations in court because he always wanted to win. It was easier to be rational and emotionally detached when someone else's future was at stake.

This time it was his life on the line. Everything was riding on the argument he was going to make.

"But no pressure," he said grimly.

Chapter Fifteen

Casey cleaned up her dad's kitchen after cooking dinner. Unlike other evenings in the two weeks since she'd come to stay with him, Nathan Thomas hung around to help. It was kind of freaking her out.

She glanced around the long, spacious room, with its oblong, white tile-topped counter and cabinets below. The refrigerator stood at one end and the nook filled with a maple dinette was at the other. Across from the kitchen was the family room with fireplace, and the adjacent living room had a corner group sofa and a flat-screen TV. Upstairs there were three bedrooms and a railing with glass below it. Her mother had never stepped foot in this house because her dad had moved the family here after her death. That he'd run from the painful memories had never occurred to Casey before.

Maybe it dawned on her now because she was here running

from pain of her own. She desperately missed Blake and hoped that she'd get over him.

Her father dried the small frying pan. "So, when are you planning to go back to work?"

"Are you trying to get rid of me?" She poured cleanser in the sink and started scrubbing.

"No."

"If I'm in the way, just say the word and I'll make other arrangements." She glanced out the window and became aware of the curtains framing it. They were lacy and see-through and not at all like her father. "When did you put up curtains?"

"You just noticed?"

"Yeah." She'd had a few things on her mind. Like how much she wished Blake could care about her.

He met her gaze and she noticed that he was a very handsome man. In his early fifties, he had silver in his brown hair and a nice smile when he used it. But what really snagged her attention was the sparkle in his blue eyes. What was up with that?

"So, Dad, lace?"

He cleared his throat. "I've been seeing someone."

"How long?" Casey asked.

"A few months. She works as a receptionist for my doctor."

Doctor? A sudden spurt of fear shot up her spine. "Are you okay?"

"Fine. I was there for my yearly physical." He shrugged. "Peg and I got to talking."

"Peg?"

"That's her name. Peg Daniels. She makes me laugh."

"You never told me," Casey accused.

"I'm telling you now. I like to laugh."

"No." Casey sighed. "That you're seeing someone."

"I didn't know how." He rested a hand on the counter, the dish towel dangling from his fingers. "But I figure if you're staying for a while, you should know, because she'll be coming around."

"I can get my own place."

"That's not what I'm saying. But if you don't want to meet her—"

"It's not that. It's just…" Casey rinsed out the sink, then turned off the water. "Maybe it is that. I'm not sure I want to see you with a woman. I guess because I never saw you with anyone but Mom. And you were never the same after she died." She glanced around the kitchen again. "You even sold the house and moved us here because living in the other place was too painful."

"It was hard," he admitted.

That was her dad. A master of understatement. "I guess it didn't help, me being a girl."

"Now why would you say that?"

"It couldn't have been easy for you, not knowing what to do with me after having boys."

Shadows swirled in his eyes. "Are you saying I wasn't there for you?"

"No, Dad. I just meant—"

"Because you'd be right."

"I would?"

"I was in my own world. That wasn't your fault, Case. It's mine. I did what a good soldier should never do. I retreated. The grief eased eventually, but by then you didn't seem to need me. And I didn't know how to be needed."

Casey's throat was thick with emotions she wasn't accustomed to letting him see. Or anyone else for that matter. She'd forgotten how to cry a long time ago. Except that one night with Blake. "It's okay, Dad."

"No, it's not. And it has to be said that you scared the crap out of me when you were hurt in Iraq."

"I'm sorry. And that was my own fault. I didn't see what I should have, because I was so focused on the fact that I was helping."

"You're not a mind reader, Casey. How could you possibly know the evil in that kid's heart?"

"I couldn't. But if I'd just kept to myself—"

"The bad stuff in the world would never get better if everyone kept to themselves," he said.

"I wish my friend's family didn't have to pay the price. Then Paula would still be alive and her kids would have their mom."

"And you know how hard it is growing up without a mom, don't you?"

She nodded. "Yeah, I do."

His eyes were sad. "I was too broken to help you, baby. But maybe Paula's kids have a better dad, one who can be there for them. Help them through it. Help them heal."

"It's okay, Daddy—" Her voice caught and she bit back a sob.

Nathan held out his arms and she walked into them. He held her and rubbed her back. "It's not okay. But I did the best I could. You haven't called me Daddy since right after your mom died."

"I guess I grew up fast."

"You'll always be my little girl. That said, what made you run home and hide with your old man?"

"It's nothing. Just taking a break from work."

He held her at arm's length, studying her. "Seems to me a break from work should make you look relaxed. And I'm not seeing it."

"Not sleeping well." A by-product of too many dreams starring Blake Decker. Sometimes she woke in the middle of the night, so lonely that there was a deep ache in the middle of her heart.

"Being tired doesn't explain the sadness in your eyes, Casey."

"It's nothing. Just burnout."

"I don't think so." Nathan folded his arms over his chest. "What's his name?"

Casey's gaze jumped to his. "How do you know it's a guy?"

"Just a guess."

"I think I liked it better when you ignored me," she grumbled.

"Not an option. There's a new sheriff in town," he said a little sheepishly.

"And her name is Peg."

"You're changing the subject." There was a determined set to his mouth.

Casey sighed. "His name is Blake Decker and he was my boss until I quit. And you know the rest."

"Like hell. What did he do?"

"All the right things." Except loving her. "He took in his orphaned niece and is learning how to be a good father to her."

"So she's all grown-up?"

"No. She's still twelve."

"Then why are you here?" His eyes narrowed. "You're in love with him."

Casey knew it wasn't a question. "He had a bad experience and isn't looking for romance."

"Neither was I, but it happens, anyway. So what are you going to do about it?"

"There's nothing to do. He's making a life with his family. I'll go on to another assignment."

"You've got more of me in you than I thought. And that's not a compliment."

"What does that mean?" Casey demanded, anger pushing away the gooey feeling from moments ago.

"You're running away, just like I did."

"What the heck?" She was no coward. It had taken guts to do what was best for everyone. "I stepped aside so he could concentrate on family. It was the right thing."

"Wrong. You retreated because you're afraid to take a chance on getting close to someone." He pointed at her. "Been there, baby. Done that. You can tell yourself you've got a halo and wings, but it doesn't fly with me. You got jacked up by letting someone close and you're running scared because you just might do it again. And this time no doctor can fix the damage."

He was right, she thought. Her life would be blown apart, not in a physical way, but it would still be devastating. Taking herself out of the game was the best way to keep from getting hurt. Except she was still hurting.

"When did you get so smart?" she asked, smiling sadly at her dad.

"If I was that bright, I'd be able to fix it. Trust me, it hurts like hell that I can't." A gleam stole into his eyes. "How about if I beat him up for you? I may not be good at talking about my feelings, but I'm pretty sure I can kick the ass of the jerk who hurt my kid."

Casey laughed even as sadness seared her heart. "I wouldn't advise that. He's an attorney and wouldn't hesitate to charge you with assault and battery."

"It would be worth it."

"Not to me." She stepped close and hugged him. "I feel like I just found you and I'd rather not lose you again. Besides, you probably wouldn't do well in prison."

"No." His chest rumbled when he laughed. "I'd miss you. And Peg."

His tone was rusty, kind of like his way of talking about feelings. But he did it for her and made her feel marginally better.

"Don't feel guilty about loving someone again, Dad."

"Okay." He rubbed his big hand up and down her back. "On one condition."

"What's that?"

"You don't feel guilty about it, either," he said.

"Deal."

And that was easy for her to promise because she had nothing on the line. She could care about Blake all she wanted and do it without guilt because he would never love her back.

After the heart-to-heart with her dad, Casey went upstairs to her room and grabbed the book on the nightstand, then flopped on the bed. But when she tried to read, her mind refused to take part in the exercise. After going over the same paragraph too many times to count, she quit.

Did her brothers know that her dad was seeing someone? If so, how come they hadn't told her? Or was it classified intelligence—as in "for men's ears only"?

She brushed her hand over the comforter on the bed and just then registered the fact that it was new. Actually she had noticed before but hadn't paid much attention until now, after finding out there was a woman in her dad's life. Casey should have realized something was up because of the homey touches in the guest room. It was all very un-Nathan-like.

The full-size bed still had the brass head- and footboards. The maple dresser and nightstands and the matching bookcase were the same, but there were pictures on the walls. Oval frames. Her dad wasn't an "oval-framed picture" man. On top of the bookcase was a wire birdcage, and the swing inside was shaped like a heart. Her dad didn't do hearts as a decorating touch. But the comforter was really out of character for him, especially because it had purple flowers and greenery, although the background was beige. That was her dad. Only better.

The more the information sank in that he wasn't alone any longer, the happier she was for him. It made her own loneliness even sadder and more pathetic.

When she'd come here after leaving Blake's, what she'd been most aware of was the comfort in this room, which had once been so depressing, and not the details that made it so inviting. She probably hadn't noticed because she was too preoccupied with missing Blake and his niece. Mia was a terrific kid. Casey even missed her abrasive sarcasm. How pathetic was that? And how much longer could this pity party go on?

She needed to get back to work because hanging out with nothing to do gave her too much time to think and play Monday-morning quarterback. To replay every minute at Blake's and wonder what she could have done differently. The fact was that he didn't feel the same as she did, and the sooner she let it go, the better off she would be.

There was a knock on her door. When she opened it, Nathan stood there. "Hi. What's up, Dad?"

"Someone is here to see you."

No one knew she was here except Ginger, who'd promised not to tell anyone. But her father was wearing an intense expression that was so much more familiar than the mooning-over-Peg face she'd seen just a while ago.

"Is there a problem?" she asked.

"That's for you to decide. I was on my way out to take Peg to a show, but I can stick around if you need me."

Her heart started pounding and the hair at her nape prickled with awareness. Blake Decker sensitivity. Something told her that that traitor Ginger Davis had broken her word.

"Is it Blake?"

"Said that's his name." If anything, her dad's expression was even more grim.

"Tell him I'm not here." As soon as the words were out of her mouth, she remembered what he'd said earlier about running home to hide.

"That won't work," he said, obviously willing to help her out. "Your car's parked in front."

"Oh. Right."

"I could tell him you don't want to see him."

If only that were true. More than anything Casey wanted to look at him just one more time. But that was pointless.

"Would you really say that?" she asked.

Nathan nodded. "But I'm not sure it would get rid of him."

"Why?"

"Instinct. A guy thing." He shrugged. "The man is on a mission and something tells me he's not leaving until he's achieved his objective."

Why was he here? It didn't make any sense. He hadn't been able to give her an answer about where she fit into his life, and she'd made it clear that settling for less than she wanted wasn't an option. There was nothing left to say.

Unless this was about Mia. Was there something wrong? Had she disappeared again? Worry gathered around her like a cloud.

She brushed past her father in the doorway. "I'll talk to him."

She walked down the stairs, turned on the landing and saw him standing just inside the front door. He was wearing the look she'd come to know—and love—so well. The tie was missing in action, but the white dress shirt was wrinkled in all the right places from a day at work, and long sleeves were rolled to mid-forearm. It made his already broad shoulders look even wider, and her pulse stuttered. His charcoal slacks were expertly tailored and fit his trim waist and muscular legs perfectly.

She held the railing when her legs started to tremble, and

managed to make it all the way into the living room without tripping.

"Hello, Blake."

"Casey."

His expression gave nothing away, so she had to ask, "What are you doing here? Is Mia all right?"

"Fine."

When his gaze moved past her, she glanced around and saw her father.

"Everything all right, Casey?" Nathan asked.

"Yeah." She glanced between the two men. "I guess introductions aren't necessary."

"No. Do you want me to stay?" her father asked.

She shook her head. "I'm fine. Be sure and tell Peg I'm looking forward to meeting her. I'd like to thank her for all the nice little touches in the guest room."

Nathan shrugged as a small smile played over his mouth. He didn't bother to deny her assumption. "I'll pass that along."

"Have a good time." Casey gave him a hug. "Love you, Dad."

"I love you, too." Nathan squeezed her back and dropped a kiss on the top of her head before walking out the door.

She looked at Blake. "If Mia's fine, I don't understand why you're here."

"You're a coward, Casey."

"What?" She hadn't expected a sneak attack.

"The first time we met, I thought you were straightforward and honest. You had more integrity in your pinkie than anyone I'd ever met. Now I know I was wrong about that."

His words stirred up anger, which crushed her self-pity. "You went to all the trouble of finding out where I was just to insult me?"

"Courage is when you go on in spite of the hard stuff. The bad stuff. But you ran away."

"I quit. There's a difference."

"Semantics," he said.

"What is this? Pick on Casey day? Who do you think you are? By definition, quitting means I don't work for you anymore. If you're determined to evaluate my job performance, you're in the wrong place. And clearly Ginger can't be trusted."

"I'm here to get through to you." He settled his hands on his lean hips and looked down for a moment. "I admit I've been hiding, not willing to take a chance on caring, because getting kicked in the teeth isn't something one willingly signs up for. But that has nothing to do with my career choice. If a couple decides to call it quits, each individual has rights that need protecting. That's what I do."

"Thanks for the clarification. I don't need protecting." Casey could almost feel her heart breaking, and the words were a brazen lie.

"I disagree, but it's hard to prove my case when you won't give me a chance." Intensity glittered in his eyes. "You're too busy punishing yourself for what happened to your friend."

The words slammed her in the chest. "You have no right to say that—"

"Sue me. Someone has to make you see that you won't let yourself be happy." He moved closer and gripped her hands. "She died because of evil you couldn't possibly comprehend. A kid blew himself up and murdered her. If you go on in this half a life, the killer gets to claim one more victim. Don't give him the satisfaction. Paula wouldn't want that."

She didn't know what to say, and even if she did, she couldn't have forced words past the lump in her throat.

Blake gently squeezed her fingers. "So, that's why I came. Every day I see people who turn their backs on love without trying to make it work. And I just wanted to say that if you're that kind of woman, you're not anyone I want to be with."

Then he dropped her hands, walked out and slammed the door.

Casey couldn't breathe, what with the pain in her chest cutting off oxygen. Then suddenly tears filled her eyes and rolled down her cheeks. In that instant she remembered why she had deliberately learned to forget how to cry. It simply hurt too much. She had no reserves to rally her defenses and stop the sob that tore up from somewhere deep inside her. She buried her face in her hands.

She didn't consciously hear the door open again, but the next thing she knew, strong arms gathered her close to a familiar and wonderful warmth.

Comfort flowed as Blake's voice washed over her. "Don't cry, Casey. Please, don't cry."

She lowered her hands and looked up at him in amazement. "You came back."

"Technically, I never left. I couldn't take the chance that you wouldn't come after me." He smiled. "This is me coming after you."

"Why?"

"I love you."

It was like the sun peeking through the clouds. "Really?"

"I guess I deserve that." He cupped her face in his palms and brushed the tears away with his thumbs. "You asked me how you were part of the family and I didn't give you a complete answer. Guess I'm a coward, too."

"Takes one to know one?" she asked.

"Something like that." His smile was fleeting. "You're the heart and soul of my family, Casey. Without you there is no family. I wish I could delete every selfish thing I ever did to convince you I couldn't love you or Mia. The truth is that I love you both. So much. I can't let you go. I won't."

"Really?"

"Really." Determination looked good on him. "Marry me, Casey. Be Mia's mom. Be my wife. If necessary you can consider that an order."

"You can't order me to love you," she said, happiness bubbling inside her.

"I know. That's not what I meant." He shook his head. "This is the worst possible time for words, which I've always counted on, to fail me. I guess it was too much to ask—"

Casey pressed a finger to his lips. "I just meant that I already love you."

"Really?" He blinked.

"I am in love with you and have been for a while."

"The implication is that you just agreed to marry me," he clarified.

"Nothing would make me happier."

He blew out a breath, then lowered his mouth to hers, a coming together of hearts and souls. A promise for the future. It was a while before they came up for air and the two of them smiled at each other.

"So is your father really going to beat me up?" he asked.

"Did he tell you that?"

He nodded and said, "Maybe he'll cut me some slack if I explain that I fell madly in love with his daughter and want to make her the happiest woman in the world."

"That will work." She slid her arms around his waist and rested her cheek on his chest. "And by the way, mission accomplished."

* * * * *

*Celebrate 60 years of pure reading pleasure
with Harlequin®!*

To commemorate the event, Silhouette Special Edition
invites you to Ashley O'Ballivan's bed-and-breakfast in
the small town of Stone Creek. The beautiful innkeeper
will have her hands full caring for her old flame Jack
McCall. He's on the run and recovering from a mysterious illness, but that won't stop him from trying to win
Ashley back.

*Enjoy an exclusive glimpse of Linda Lael Miller's
AT HOME IN STONE CREEK
Available in November 2009
from Silhouette Special Edition®*

The helicopter swung abruptly sideways in a dizzying arch, setting Jack McCall's fever-ravaged brain spinning.

His friend's voice sounded tinny, coming through the earphones. "You belong in a hospital," he said. "Not some backwater bed-and-breakfast."

All Jack really knew about the virus raging through his system was that it wasn't contagious, and there was no known treatment for it besides a lot of rest and quiet. "I don't like hospitals," he responded, hoping he sounded like his normal self. "They're full of sick people."

Vince Griffin chuckled but it was a dry sound, rough at the edges. "What's in Stone Creek, Arizona?" he asked. "Besides a whole lot of nothin'?"

Ashley O'Ballivan was in Stone Creek, and she was a whole lot of somethin', but Jack had neither the strength nor the inclination to explain. After the way he'd ducked out six months before, he didn't expect a welcome, knew he didn't deserve one. But Ashley, being Ashley, would take him in whatever her misgivings.

He had to get to Ashley; he'd be all right.

He closed his eyes, letting the fever swallow him.

There was no telling how much time had passed when he became aware of the chopper blades slowing overhead. Dimly, he saw the private ambulance waiting on the airfield outside of Stone Creek; it seemed that twilight had descended.

Jack sighed with relief. His clothes felt clammy against his flesh. His teeth began to chatter as two figures unloaded a gurney from the back of the ambulance and waited for the blades to stop.

"Great," Vince remarked, unsnapping his seat belt. "Those two look like volunteers, not real EMTs."

The chopper bounced sickeningly on its runners, and Vince, with a shake of his head, pushed open his door and jumped to the ground, head down.

Jack waited, wondering if he'd be able to stand on his own. After fumbling unsuccessfully with the buckle on his seat belt, he decided not.

When it was safe the EMTs approached, following Vince, who opened Jack's door.

His old friend Tanner Quinn stepped around Vince, his grin not quite reaching his eyes.

"You look like hell warmed over," he told Jack cheerfully.

"Since when are you an EMT?" Jack retorted.

Tanner reached in, wedged a shoulder under Jack's right arm and hauled him out of the chopper. His knees immediately buckled, and Vince stepped up, supporting him on the other side.

"In a place like Stone Creek," Tanner replied, "everybody helps out."

They reached the wheeled gurney, and Jack found himself on his back.

Tanner and the second man strapped him down, a process that brought back a few bad memories.

"Is there even a hospital in this place?" Vince asked irritably from somewhere in the night.

"There's a pretty good clinic over in Indian Rock," Tanner answered easily, "and it isn't far to Flagstaff." He paused to help his buddy hoist Jack and the gurney into the back of the ambulance. "You're in good hands, Jack. My wife is the best veterinarian in the state."

Jack laughed raggedly at that.

Vince muttered a curse.

Tanner climbed into the back beside him, perched on some kind of fold-down seat. The other man shut the doors.

"You in any pain?" Tanner said as his partner climbed into the driver's seat and started the engine.

"No." Jack looked up at his oldest and closest friend and wished he'd listened to Vince. Ever since he'd come down with the virus—a week after snatching a five-year-old girl back from her non-custodial parent, a small-time Colombian drug dealer—he hadn't been able to think about anyone or anything but Ashley. When he *could* think, anyway.

Now, in one of the first clearheaded moments he'd experienced since checking himself out of Bethesda the day before, he realized he might be making a major mistake. Not by facing Ashley—he owed her that much and a lot more. No, he could be putting her in danger, putting Tanner and his daughter and his pregnant wife in danger, too.

"I shouldn't have come here," he said, keeping his voice low.

Tanner shook his head, his jaw clamped down hard as though he was irritated by Jack's statement.

"This is where you belong," Tanner insisted. "If you'd had

sense enough to know that six months ago, old buddy, when you bailed on Ashley without so much as a fare-thee-well, you wouldn't be in this mess."

Ashley. The name had run through his mind a million times in those six months, but hearing somebody say it out loud was like having a fist close around his insides and squeeze hard.

Jack couldn't speak.

Tanner didn't press for further conversation.

The ambulance bumped over country roads, finally hitting smooth blacktop.

"Here we are," Tanner said. "Ashley's place."

* * * * *

Will Jack be able to patch things up with Ashley,
or will his past put the woman he loves in harm's way?
Find out in
AT HOME IN STONE CREEK
by Linda Lael Miller
Available November 2009
from Silhouette Special Edition®

**This November,
Silhouette Special Edition®
brings you**

NEW YORK TIMES
BESTSELLING AUTHOR

LINDA LAEL MILLER

At Home in
Stone Creek

*Available in November
wherever books are sold.*

HARLEQUIN Romance.

This November,
queen of the rugged rancher

PATRICIA THAYER

teams up with

DONNA ALWARD

to bring you an extra-special treat
this holiday season—

two romantic stories
in one book!

Join sisters Amelia and Kelley for Christmas at
Rocking H Ranch where these feisty cowgirls swap
presents for proposals, mistletoe for marriage and
experience the unbeatable rush of falling in love!

Available in November wherever books are sold.

www.eHarlequin.com

HRI7619

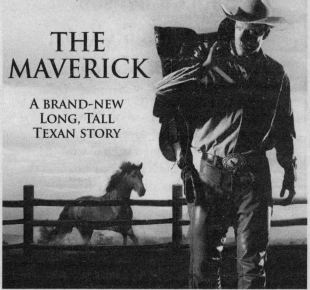

Silhouette Desire

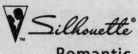

Silhouette®

Romantic
SUSPENSE

**Sparked by Danger,
Fueled by Passion.**

---

*Blackout
At Christmas*

Beth Cornelison,
Sharron McClellan,
Jennifer Morey

What happens when a major blackout shuts
down the entire Western seaboard on Christmas
Eve? Follow stories of danger, intrigue and
romance as three women learn to trust their
instincts to survive and open their hearts to the
love that unexpectedly comes their way.

**Available November
wherever books are sold.**

SRS27653

REQUEST YOUR FREE BOOKS!

2 FREE NOVELS PLUS 2 FREE GIFTS!

Silhouette®

SPECIAL EDITION®

Life, Love and Family!

YES! Please send me 2 FREE Silhouette Special Edition® novels and my 2 FREE gifts (gifts are worth about $10). After receiving them, if I don't wish to receive any more books, I can return the shipping statement marked "cancel." If I don't cancel, I will receive 6 brand-new novels every month and be billed just $4.24 per book in the U.S. or $4.99 per book in Canada. That's a savings of at least 15% off the cover price! It's quite a bargain! Shipping and handling is just 50¢ per book.* I understand that accepting the 2 free books and gifts places me under no obligation to buy anything. I can always return a shipment and cancel at any time. Even if I never buy another book from Silhouette, the two free books and gifts are mine to keep forever.

235 SDN EYN4 335 SDN EYPG

Name _____ (PLEASE PRINT)

Address _____ Apt. #

City _____ State/Prov. _____ Zip/Postal Code

Signature (if under 18, a parent or guardian must sign)

Mail to the **Silhouette Reader Service:**
IN U.S.A.: P.O. Box 1867, Buffalo, NY 14240-1867
IN CANADA: P.O. Box 609, Fort Erie, Ontario L2A 5X3

Not valid to current subscribers of Silhouette Special Edition books.

Want to try two free books from another line?
Call 1-800-873-8635 or visit www.morefreebooks.com.

* Terms and prices subject to change without notice. Prices do not include applicable taxes. Sales tax applicable in N.Y. Canadian residents will be charged applicable provincial taxes and GST. Offer not valid in Quebec. This offer is limited to one order per household. All orders subject to approval. Credit or debit balances in a customer's account(s) may be offset by any other outstanding balance owed by or to the customer. Please allow 4 to 6 weeks for delivery. Offer available while quantities last.

Your Privacy: Silhouette is committed to protecting your privacy. Our Privacy Policy is available online at www.eHarlequin.com or upon request from the Reader Service. From time to time we make our lists of customers available to reputable third parties who may have a product or service of interest to you. If you would prefer we not share your name and address, please check here. ☐

SSE09R

HARLEQUIN
Ambassadors

Want to share your passion for reading Harlequin® Books?

Become a Harlequin Ambassador!

Harlequin Ambassadors are a group of passionate and well-connected readers who are willing to share their joy of reading Harlequin® books with family and friends.

You'll be sent all the tools you need to spark great conversation, including free books!

All we ask is that you share the romance with your friends and family!

You'll also be invited to have a say in new book ideas and exchange opinions with women just like you!

To see if you qualify* to be a Harlequin Ambassador, please visit www.HarlequinAmbassadors.com.

*Please note that not everyone who applies to be a Harlequin Ambassador will qualify. For more information please visit www.HarlequinAmbassadors.com.

Thank you for your participation.

BAP09BPA

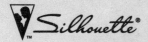
Silhouette®

SPECIAL EDITION

COMING NEXT MONTH
Available October 27, 2009

#2005 AT HOME IN STONE CREEK—Linda Lael Miller
Sometimes Ashley O'Ballivan felt like the only single woman left in
Stone Creek. All because of security expert Jack McCall—the man
who broke her heart years ago. Now Jack was mysteriously back in
town…and Ashley's single days were numbered.

#2006 A LAWMAN FOR CHRISTMAS—Marie Ferrarella
Kate's Boys
When a car accident landed her mother in the hospital, it
was Kelsey Marlowe's worst nightmare. Luckily, policeman
Morgan Donnelly was there to save her mom, and the nightmare
turned into a dream come true—as Kelsey fell hard for the sexy
lawman!

#2007 QUINN McCLOUD'S CHRISTMAS BRIDE—
Lois Faye Dyer
The McClouds of Montana
Wolf Creek's temporary sheriff Quinn McCloud was a wanderer;
librarian Abigail Foster was the type to set down roots. But when
they joined forces to help a little girl left on Abigail's doorstep, did
opposites ever attract! And just in time for a Christmas wedding.

#2008 THE TEXAN'S DIAMOND BRIDE—Teresa Hill
The Foleys and the McCords
When Travis Foley caught gemologist Paige McCord snooping
around on his property for the fabled Santa Magdalena Diamond, it
spelled trouble for the feuding families. But what was it about this
irresistible interloper that gave the rugged rancher pause?

#2009 MERRY CHRISTMAS, COWBOY!—Cindy Kirk
Meet Me in Montana
All academic Lauren Van Meveren wanted from her trip to Big Sky
country was peace and quiet to write her dissertation. But when
she moved onto widower Seth Anderssen's ranch to help with his
daughter, Lauren got the greatest gift of all—true love.

#2010 MOONLIGHT AND MISTLETOE—Dawn Temple
When her estranged father sent Beverly Hills attorney
Kyle Anderson to strong-arm her into a settlement, Shayna Miller
was determined to resist…until Kyle melted her heart and had her
heading for the nearest mistletoe, head-over-heels in love….